POINTED HATS bobbing over old-hag faces, broomsticks, and long black swishy dresses—such are the badges of the small witches who scurry about on Halloween, crying "Trick or treat!"

Witches are part of the Halloween fun. But not long ago—in some places even now—people really believed in witches—aged women who ride broomsticks, cast evil spells, and change themselves into black cats.

Witch hunts and cruel witch trials now belong to the past . . . but the superstitions of magic persist. In many parts of the world one still finds a lingering belief in witches, enchantments and spells.

13 Witches brings together tales from England, The Netherlands, Serbia, and other countries. So look about sharply! The 13 witches are there, to chill your spine and make you shiver.

13 WITCHES

2 Wizards, the Devil and a
Pack of Goblins

3 WITCHES

2 Wizards, the Devil
and a Pack of Goblins

by

DOROTHY GLADYS SPICER

illustrated by Sofia

COWARD-McCANN, Inc.   NEW YORK

my very dear
MIENTJE

Second Impression

© 1963 by Dorothy Gladys Spicer

Library of Congress Catalog Card Number: 63-10172

Manufactured in the United States of America

CONTENTS

ABOUT WITCHES, ENCHANTMENTS, AND SPELLS

Pointed hats bobbing over old-hag faces, broomsticks, and long black swishy dresses—such are the badges of the small witches who scurry about on Halloween, crying, "Trick or treat!"

To American boys and girls, witches are part of the Halloween fun. But not long ago—in some places even now—people really believed in witches—aged women who ride broomsticks, cast evil spells, and changed themselves into black cats.

Witch hunts and cruel witch trials now belong to the past . . . but the superstitions of magic persist. In many parts of the world one still finds a lingering belief in witches, enchantments, and spells.

"An old witch lives in yonder hill," claim some, pointing to an ancient earthwork. Or, of a lonely cross they whisper, "*That* saved a robber's soul from the Devil." Or again, they say of an enchanted slope, where a huge upright stone stands apart, "That is a Danish King. There he must remain, until the spell breaks on Judgment Day."

Long ago I learned that a story always lurks behind such talk. So—when thinking of witches—I drew on the memories of the very old. Some related strange events they'd heard in their youth. Others led me to the scenes of eerie events. The stories I am telling you are based on such things.

13 Witches brings together tales from England, The Netherlands, Serbia, and other lands. One day you, too, may visit these countries. And when you do, you may hear stories of the witches —good and bad—who glide through the mist, and haunt old places! Maybe you'll see them and maybe you won't—*but folks say they are there,* to chill your spine and make you shiver. So look about sharply! You *may* run across some of my *13 Witches* in these tales of magic, enchantments, and spells.

DOROTHY GLADYS SPICER

9

THE YELLOW-HAIRED WITCH

(Serbia)

Long, long ago, in the land of the ancient Serbs, there lived a young Prince named Rado. Each day at dawn he left his father's palace to hunt wild boars in the mountain, or to stalk deer in the forest park. Back at the palace, after they had dined, he plucked the single string of his *goussle,* and sang to his father, the King.

Rado's favorite ballad was about a prince who rode a black horse. As the steed flew along on wing-swift feet, the prince hurled his sword into the clouds, then caught it in his hand. Oh, the prince and his horse did marvelous things, and Rado loved to recite their exploits.

One night Rado reached for his goussle as usual, and started to sing. He told how the horse scaled a cliff, while his master rescued a maid in distress. Then they rode off on a further adventure. At first the King listened with interest. Then he stirred in his chair and raised a jeweled finger.

"Stop, my son, stop!" he commanded. "Don't you ever weary of the chase, of your songs of this prince and his wonderful deeds? I, your father, am heavy with age. In a year and a day you will be a man. You must lay aside childish things. You must learn affairs of state. But first, find a wife. Only when you are settled can I die in peace."

In dismay, Rado dropped his goussle. The single string snapped with a twang.

"Father," he protested, *"I don't want a wife!* I am happy with you—with things as they are."

The King rose from his seat. He pounded the table until the red wine danced in the golden goblets.

"Things never remain as they are forever," he thundered. "Tomorrow your horse will await you at the palace gate. You will journey into the world to look for a princess. Bring your bride back to the palace, my son, a year and a day from this night."

The King, who refused to listen to the Prince's protests and pleas, drew a purse from his bosom.

"Here is gold," he said, "enough for your needs. Return to the palace at the appointed time, and all will be well. If you fail to heed my wishes, your sorrow will be great. I shall banish you forever to a distant land.''

When Rado saw that nothing would change the King's mind, he bid his father farewell. In the gray light of dawn he rode away sadly, to seek the bride he didn't want.

During the weeks that followed, Rado journeyed far. He looked upon many fair faces. But whenever he tried to woo a girl, something was always wrong. This princess was too fat, that one too thin. Another argued—or else agreed to everything he said.

The weeks slipped into months. Still Rado had found no princess to his liking.

"I'd rather die than marry a girl I can't ever love," he exclaimed one day, riding his horse in the mountains that skirted his father's kingdom. "But what can I do? My gold is now gone. So is my time. In three days, my father expects me back with a bride. And if I fail—"

Rado choked at the thought of the old King's anger, of the exile and disgrace that awaited him. So great was his misery that the Prince did not notice where his horse took him. He did not even look about until the animal stopped. Then, as he stared up at a mountain that rose before them, bleak and grim, a desperate thought took shape in his mind.

The Prince slipped from his saddle. He threw his arms about the neck of his horse, then buried his face in the tawny mane.

"Go home to my father," he sobbed. "Everything is finished for me. I have not found a bride and I cannot endure exile forever. I have no other choice."

The horse gazed at his master, who embraced him once more. Then Rado tightened his belt and started up the mountain without glancing back.

From the top he studied a torrent that foamed and swirled over black jagged rocks far below.

"It is the only way," the Prince whispered.

He glanced up at the blue sky. He gulped in the clean cold air, then raised his arms and prepared to jump.

"Stop, stop!" cried a voice sharply, from somewhere behind.

Rado turned, but saw no one. Again he made ready to leap.

"*Stop!*" the voice ordered, the second time. "If you destroy your own life, it can do *you* no good. Besides, you will be killing three-score other young men."

The Prince peered this way and that, but still could not see the owner of the voice.

"Come out of hiding, whoever you are," cried Rado. "If you knew my troubles, you would hardly jest."

"I *do* know your troubles, my son," said the voice. "But others have troubles, too."

All at once a little bent man stood before the unhappy Prince. The stranger was wrinkled and old. His long white beard touched the tip of his toes.

"Do you see yonder mountain?" the old man asked, pointing to an adjoining peak.

Rado nodded.

"On the very top," the stranger continued, "a witch sits, night and day. She has long yellow hair, but don't let *that* fool you! She is old—very old, my son. Chained to her hand is a small green bird. Free it, and you'll be the happiest man in the land."

"My happiness is gone forever," said Rado, sighing.

He turned his back on the old man and stared again at the rushing torrent.

"Tut, tut," the ancient exclaimed. "You're a stubborn youth. Climb to the top of the mountain and set the bird free. Once you vanquish the old hag, you'll restore to life the young princes, now sleeping in stones at her feet."

"How can I free the bird?" Rado asked, interested now despite his resolve to die.

"You must creep up behind the witch," the old man replied, "and seize her yellow hair. But mind you, lad, don't let her see *you,* or she'll turn you to stone. Once you hold her tresses, don't let go— no matter what happens. Only so, can you save the bird and help the princes."

So speaking, the stranger vanished.

The Prince thought it all over.

"I'll climb the mountain," he decided finally. "If I can't take the witch by surprise, I am no worse off than now. Either way, I'll die. And who knows—with luck there may yet be a chance!"

Rado strode toward the mountain. The going was rough. The rocks were jagged and sharp. Painfully the young Prince inched along. It was dawn of the third day before he reached the top.

There the Prince stopped and caught his breath. On a rock, not three rods away, sat the witch. Her back was toward Rado. Over her shoulders fell her long yellow hair, as bright and thick as any

13

young girl's. A small green bird, captive on a chain, struggled and fluttered at her wrist. Whenever the witch stroked its feathers with her long finger, the tiny creature shrank in fear.

Holding his breath, Rado crept forward. Great stones lay scattered all about on the ground. They're the princes, he thought. If the old hag sees me before I get hold of her hair—

Rado reached out a hand. The witch, hearing a twig snap, started to turn her head. The Prince sprang forward and grasped her locks. The witch shuddered and shook. She tried to wrench herself free, then began to shriek.

She struggled and yelled until the mountain trembled. Leaves dropped from the trees. Stones rocked in their beds.

"Leave me be!" screamed the witch. "Let go of my hair!"

"That I'll not do," declared Rado.

"Let go, you fool," howled the old woman. "What do you want with me?"

"Two things," answered Rado, with a nasty jerk. "Give me the green bird that perches on your wrist, and—"

"*Never!*" cried the witch.

"Restore life to the princes who sleep in these stones."

The witch squirmed and twisted, then tried to slither from Rado's grasp. The more she struggled the tighter he held her. At last she said craftily, "All right, young man. You drive a hard bargain. Let go, and I'll do as you say."

Rado answered with a tug that lifted the writhing creature off her rock, and almost sent him sprawling. But he never loosened his grip.

Then the witch screamed until the sky turned black. Lizards hurried to shelter. Birds hid their heads under their wings.

"I'm done for," moaned the yellow-haired witch. "Done for forever, robbed of my power, tricked by a silly youth."

Reluctantly she unchained the bird. The small trembling creature flew to Rado's shoulder.

Then the witch muttered and cursed with such terrible words that Rado covered his ears. The mountain heaved and groaned. Rumblings came from inside the earth. Uttering a blood-curdling howl, the witch disappeared in black smoke. After that there was deep silence.

Rado did not know how long the blackness continued. At last the sun came out. The little birds sang. The whole mountain seemed to come to life. Then *the threescore stones turned into threescore young men.*

They pressed about Rado with shouts of gratitude.

"Dear Prince, you have freed us from the witch's evil spell," they cried. "We shall serve you gladly as long as we live."

"You can serve me best, kind friends, by going home to your loved ones," said Rado, gazing at the eager young faces. "*They* think you dead."

The princes grasped Rado's hand and thanked him. When they had bounded down the mountainside, the little bird flew from his shoulder. She shook her bright feathers. At once she was transformed into a beautiful Princess, all April in her deep blue eyes. As the young man gazed into them, he knew that here was the one woman he loved.

He took her into his arms and kissed her tenderly.

"The wicked one stole me as a child from my father," explained the Princess. "She turned me into a bird. Later she chained me to her wrist. Those threescore princes tried in vain to free me. But you alone knew how to destroy the witch's power. Were it not for you, the princes would still be stones, and I an unhappy green bird."

Rado then told the Princess about the old man of the mountain, how *he* had revealed the secret for overcoming the yellow-haired witch. Talking thus, the hours slipped away—until Rado remembered this was the night of his tryst with the King.

"What shall we do?" he cried in dispair. "At midnight it will be a year and a day since I left the palace. By midnight we must be there. I must present you to my father, but we are far from home."

"Never fear, beloved," said the Princess. She drew a wand from her bosom. "This magic wand will help us. I took it one night from the old witch as she slept. When she wakened and discovered what I had done, she changed me into a bird."

Rado tucked the wand into his belt. Hand-in-hand, the lovers hurried down the mountain. When they came to the torrent where Rado had planned to die, he touched the eddying waters with his wand. They parted at once. The Prince and the Princess walked over dry ground to a green grassy slope opposite.

Bluebells and primroses sprang under their feet. Larks flew skyward from nests in the grass. It was spring in the meadow, but soon Rado and his Princess entered a dark forest. Dense trees shut out the sunlight. Spindly-legged spiders danced from gnarled limbs. Wolves howled like demons in the distance. Closer and closer their cries

16

came. Before many minutes the two saw black monster shapes bounding through the trees.

"The wand! The wand!" cried the Princess, as a huge wolf leaped toward them.

Rado lifted the wand. Instantly the howling pack turned and fled into the shadows.

As Rado and the Princess emerged from the forest, a horse with a tawny mane galloped toward them. With loud whinnies the creature rushed up to Rado.

"Faithful friend," cried the Prince, rubbing his horse's nose. "Take us home by midnight—home to my father, the King."

Rado swung into the saddle, then lifted the Princess before him. Away they flew at breathless speed, across meadows and hills and rich fertile valleys.

At last horse and riders clattered into the city of the King. No light shone from the windows, no man roamed the streets. The chimes in the church belfry had started to strike.

"It is midnight," whispered Rado in his horse's ear. "Hurry, my beauty, to the palace with haste."

The horse raced like the wind through the black empty streets. His tawny tail floated behind, like a banner of silk.

Nine, ten, eleven, *twelve,* chimed the bells, just as the horse bounded through the palace gates. The old King stood there waiting in his rich purple robes. He pressed Rado and his Princess close to his breast.

The next night, after the wedding, Rado reached for his goussle. He mended the broken string, then sang his own story to his father. He sang of a princess, with the sweet face of spring, whom a yellow-haired witch had turned into a bird. Then he related how Rado, a foolish young prince, met an old man on the mountain. He helped him free the princess, and restore threescore youths to life.

"Rado brought his bride home," chanted the Prince in conclusion. "There they lived forever after, with Rado the happiest man in the land."

"This song," said the King, when Rado had finished, "I shall never tire of hearing. Sing it again, my son!"

THE MAGIC MOUNTAIN
(Czechoslovakia)

The Bible tells us that strange things happened on Good Friday, the day that Jesus died for our sins. At noon the sky grew black as night. The earth trembled. The temple curtain split in two.

For hundreds of years—on this same awful day—strange things have happened in the Bohemian hills. Those who find the Magic Mountain before sunrise can see the rocks burst open, and behold the treasure of gold inside.

Long ago, Annie, a village widow, found this treasure, but lost something far more precious. Today no one knows where the Mountain is. But many believe it exists. They say an evil witch piles her gold there, to tempt people like Annie to sin.

Annie was a pretty young woman. She lived alone with her baby in a cottage with a scrap of garden behind. Annie scrubbed for a living. She baked for village housewives. She was poor, but her goat gave milk for the child. There was always meal in her bin. Annie had all she needed, yet—like many who have enough—she always wanted more.

"If I could only buy that flowered shawl for my head," Annie would sigh when she went to the fair. Or, "The baby would look sweet in that ruffled bonnet—but her old one will have to do." Or Annie would lift a feast bread from a customer's oven and say, "So many raisins, eggs, and almonds, all in one loaf. These things would last *me* a year!"

Annie's greed and envy increased each day. She pined for laces. She longed for a velvet bodice with red roses on it. She wanted ribbons for her hair, and a coral necklace with a real gold clasp.

"Your mother would be the prettiest woman in the village, with decent clothes on her back," Annie would tell the baby. "Then things would be different for you, little treasure. Soon you'd have a father again!"

Annie's resentment deepened as the Easter Feast drew near. During Lent nobody wore fine clothes. Nobody ate rich foods. But after Passion Week, all the village girls would bloom like flowers in the spring.

Tomorrow will be Green Thursday, the day Jesus washed His Disciples' feet, thought Annie as she cleaned a kitchen floor. *I'll be*

scrubbing for other people. I'll be making lamb cakes, sticking in raisin eyes, tying blue bows on their silly necks!

Through the window Annie heard the children chanting from door to door,

> *Tomorrow's Green Thursday*
> *When we bake the lamb*
> *And eat our cakes*
> *With honey.*

"Fine foods for all but Annie," grumbled the widow from her knees.

She slopped water behind the tile stove. A hen clucked and flew toward the door.

"Annie can scrub her fingers to the bone," muttered the woman as she worked, "while others feast and show off their fine clothes."

The next evening, while feeding the baby warm goat's milk, a wonderful idea popped into Annie's mind. In her excitement she almost dropped the child.

"Tomorrow will be Great Friday!" cried Annie. "How could I forget? On that day, my granny used to tell me, the Magic Mountain opens and shows all of the treasure within."

The mother ran her fingers through the child's soft curls, then wiped the dimpled chin.

"When I was small," Annie told her, "and you, little flower, unborn, my granny often told me the story, just as her elders had told it to her.

" 'That is the Magic Mountain,' she would say, pointing across the meadow. 'A witch lives inside. Nobody has ever seen her. But there in the Mountain she busily counts her gold.' "

The widow laid the child on the cot, for now the soft lids were fluttering over the bluebell eyes.

"I can hear Granny's very words," Annie continued, as she paced the narrow room. " 'On Good Friday, go to the Mountain before the sun is up. If you are lucky, and find the right place, the rocks will open. Then you will see the gold. Take all your hands will hold, child, and *run*. If the sun rises when you are not looking, the rocks will shut you in. *Then you must stay there forever,* locked up with the witch and her gold.' "

Annie stopped her pacing. She gazed down at the baby, pink and smiling in sleep.

"Tomorrow we'll get up early," she whispered. "We'll visit

the Magic Mountain. Then, little pet, we shall learn if Granny's story is true."

As the widow lay down she kept thinking of the gold. Gold for her child's clothes and food. Gold for her baby's dowry. Gold for sparkling jewels. Women would stare in envy when *she* swept down the street! And the men, young and old, ah, the men. . . . So Annie drifted into slumber, dreaming of gold.

Soon after midnight she woke. Moonlight streamed over the cot. The baby's curls gleamed like a halo about the chubby face.

"My little angel," murmured Annie, wrapping her in a worn shawl. "Soon you'll be rich!"

With the child pressed against her bosom, Annie crept through the sleeping village. She had never imagined silence so deep. Not a cock crowed. Not a dog barked. Shivering in the sharp wind that blew from the Mountain, the woman hugged the baby closer.

The little one seemed heavier as Annie crossed the meadow. She wanted to rest, but thought of the treasure made her burden lighter.

At last the Mountain loomed before Annie.

"So this is the Magic Mountain," she whispered in awe. She studied the great gray rocks that seemed to meet the sky.

Annie glanced at the baby, asleep in her arms.

"I'll lay you here on the grass," she said softly, "while I discover where the Mountain parts."

The widow peered on this side, then on that. She searched the rough surface up and down. With both hands she felt the rocks, but nowhere could she find a crack.

"Where *can* the opening be?" she cried in dismay. "I still have time—plenty of time," she added, scanning the dark sky.

Then the rocks split apart with a grinding crash. Annie sank to her knees in terror, for a blinding light burst through the gloom. At first she covered her eyes, unable to endure the brightness. When she could look again, Annie saw piles and piles of gold in the open Mountain.

"Oh—oh—ooo!" she gasped, unable to believe her eyes. "The Mountain is lined with gold!"

Stooping down, Annie gathered all the coins her apron would hold. She stared at the glowing mass with greedy eyes.

"There is plenty more for the taking," she murmured. "If I only had that empty jug at home!"

The widow glanced at the sky, then at the baby. Sunrise is

21

still far away, she thought. There *is* time to fetch the jug, and return for the child and the treasure. I'll travel more swiftly alone.

She knotted her apron together, then started home. The gold pieces were heavy, but the woman didn't care. With a jugful of coins beside these, she would be rich beyond dreams.

At home Annie emptied her riches into an empty crock. The sky was gray as she rushed from the village. The cock started to crow.

"Dear heaven," whispered Annie, "what shall I do if the sun rises before I get back?"

In her haste and fear the widow tripped over a root. She got up quickly and ran on faster than before. As she neared the Mountain, she could see the gold twinkling like a hundred thousand stars. Then a crash shook the earth. The rocks thundered shut. The sun rose above the Mountain.

"My baby!" cried Annie.

She stumbled forward. *Her child had disappeared!* The rocks had swallowed her, along with the gold. Annie beat with her fists until her hands were bleeding and torn.

"What good is the gold without my darling?" she wailed.

Back in the village that morning, Annie knelt in the church. She wept loudly as the priest read of Christ's Passion.

"She mourns the dead Lord," the villagers said.

Only later did they learn Annie had lost her baby. The widow never told anyone—not even the priest—what had really happened.

"She drowned in the river while I was washing clothes," she lied.

Everyone pitied Annie. They gave her more work. Mothers sent their children with gifts of cakes and eggs, sometimes a butter pat, or a plump chicken for the pot. In spite of so much kindness, Annie wept day and night. She could not bear the sight of the gold in the crock. She was rich now, but never spent a coin.

"All the treasure in the world can't pay for my baby," she cried. "When Great Friday comes, I'll take back the gold, and beg the witch for my little one."

The months passed slowly, but at last it was Green Thursday. The fragrance of lamb cakes baking in every oven made the village smell like a vast pastry shop. Everyone except Annie felt joy in the approaching feast. Her guilt and fear lest she never see her child again burdened Annie so that she couldn't sleep.

At midnight she rose. She tied the coins in her apron, then set out for the Mountain. They were heavier now than when she had

22

carried them home. It was still dark when the widow reached the Magic Mountain, grim against the sky.

"My darling has been locked within those horrible rocks a whole year," cried Annie, unable to see for tears. Later she could not remember all that happened. There were deafening crackings and crashings—those she recalled. Then for a long time, she lay still as the dead.

When she came to her senses, the meadow was warm and golden although the sky was like lead. Annie *thought* she heard music. She was never sure. The only thing she *knew* was that her baby lay there on the Mountain, cooing and kicking her tiny feet. Her soft curls framed her pink dimpled face.

"Thank you, thank you, Witch of the Mountain," cried Annie, rushing forward and clasping the child to her bosom. "You have returned my baby. I am returning your treasure. *Mine* is here in my arms."

Later that day, Annie confessed her sin to the priest. She told how the Witch of the Mountain had restored her little one.

On Easter Sunday, the day Jesus rose from the dead, Annie's heart was filled with peace.

Easter has come.
Let all rejoice
And praise our Risen Lord,

she sang with her neighbors.

When the baby smiled and twined her soft arms about her neck, Annie knew she was rich. Never again did she long for things only gold can buy. The widow prospered, for she scrubbed as she never had scrubbed before. She hummed as she worked. She envied no one, now that she had her child again.

23

THE WHITE WITCH OF ESPELOO

(Netherlands)

The River Yssel, a branch of the Rhine, meanders through East Netherlands and empties into Yssel Lake. Along its banks are towns and castles, and belfries with ancient chimes. There are also farms and woodlands, and pastures bright with buttercups and daisies.

Oh, the Yssel is a shining river, with crystal-clear waters as far as Windesheim. There the Yssel grows squalid. There the White Witch perished, a long time ago. White was her name, but black her soul. That is why, round Windesheim, the river is so dark.

The White Witch was wicked, and it's a fine thing she is dead. For in the olden days she tempted men, and led them into sin. She showered them with her riches, then refused to let them go. That is what she did to Gait—once an honest youth.

The White Witch lived in a sand cave, close to Holten Hill. Espeloo, they call the place, and you can see it yet. Gait's farm was in the neighborhood. He was a merry peasant, with a heart as light as down, and a whistle on his lips. From dawn to dark Gait tilled his land. He raised onions and potatoes. He grew purple cabbages in long straight rows. And on his trees hung apples, red and large and sweet.

On market day Gait piled his cart with produce, then jogged away to the village where his dear Golinda lived. Although he sold all he could raise, Gait never saved a copper. There was such need of seed for the earth, of fodder for the beasts, that the florins never jingled for long in Gait's old leather purse.

For all his frugal living, Gait was happy and content. He never dreamed that he was poor, until the day he asked for Golinda's hand.

"Never," cried her father, the richest farmer for miles about. "Never, until you have enough money to provide for her every wish. Golinda has her pick of half a dozen wealthy suitors. Why settle for a man who's never saved a cent?"

Gait blanched to the roots of his curly fair hair. *Not marry Golinda!* There had never been another girl for him. Since they had won that skating match as children, Gait and Golinda had known that they would wed.

The girl's father studied Gait's stricken face. He knocked out his pipe. He cleared his throat, then spoke in a kinder tone.

"I always liked you, lad, and my Golinda has, too. But love alone can't make a marriage. Without wood, the fire burns to ash. Without money, love flies out the window."

Gait could bear no more. He didn't even want to see Golinda. Choking back his tears, he ran from the house. He untied his waiting horse. He climbed into the saddle. With shoulders sagging in dejection, Gait started home.

The horse plodded along, with no word from his master. Dusk was falling as they entered the beech wood. The owls were flitting from tree to tree. *To-whoo-hoo-hoo-oo*, shrieked the birds, flapping their huge wings. Gait's heart was so heavy he didn't hear their dismal hoots. He didn't see the gray mist slowly rising from the ground.

To-whoo-whoo, called the birds through the fog.

Gait's horse couldn't see an inch in front of him, but he knew the way home through blackest night. His master, slumped in the saddle, saw nothing except Golinda's lovely face.

"I'll die, my darling," Gait cried in anguish, "unless I win you for my wife."

The thought of life without Golinda almost broke his heart. Beads of sweat stood out on his brow.

"Golinda, Golinda," sobbed the youth, "to get the gold I need to win you, I'd gladly steal, murder—even sell my soul!"

"Would you, Gait?" The question came tauntingly through the mist. *"Would* you sell your soul for Golinda?"

Gait raised his head for the first time. He jerked his horse to a halt. He stared into the fog that swirled in restless waves about the creature's feet.

"I can help you." The voice was silken now. "You have only to follow me, Gait . . . to follow me."

The youth leaned forward in the saddle. He peered through the mist. He could see no one. Suddenly the horse shied and tried to bolt through the gloom. But now Gait saw a white hand reach out through the fog and grasp the bridle. A ghostly figure appeared at the horse's head.

"Who are you?" Gait demanded sharply, fear prickling at his spine.

"I am the Witch of Espeloo," the wraith replied. "I ride

through the air on the mist. Come to my cave in the sand hill and I will give you gold—gold enough so you can wed."

"The White Witch!" exclaimed Gait, a shudder shaking his body.

As a lad, his grandfather had warned him of this creature.

"She'll come to you in the fog, boy. She'll tempt you when you are sad and alone."

Gait could hear the old man's words, as if it were yesterday.

"Never follow the White Witch, for she is evil. You'll rue the day, if you do. She gives young men gold and riches, but takes away more than she gives."

Remembering his grandfather's words, Gait urged his horse ahead. But the white hand still held the bridle. The animal did not move.

"Gold . . . gold . . . so you can wed," the White Witch whispered.

The words seared into Gait's brain. They melted his resolve to get away. He followed the witch through the mist of the beech wood. He followed her to her cave in the sand hill. It was then that he saw the gold.

It glittered like a thousand suns in the sky. Even the mist that brooded around it turned to a golden haze. The treasure sang to Gait's tortured soul. The words that it sang were these:

> *Gold for Golinda!*
> *Golinda's gold.*
> *Yours for the taking . . .*
> *To lay at her feet.*
> *Yours for Golinda,*
> *The maiden sweet.*

Gait could not recall later all the promises he had to make in exchange for the gold. But, in the end, the White Witch gave it to him and let him go.

Then he married Golinda and the wedding feast lasted three days. Everyone rejoiced. Gait was a handsome bridegroom and Golinda a lovely bride. Her golden curls shimmered beneath her white lace cap. Her eyes were like bluebells touched with dew.

The couple settled on Gait's old farm. The youth loved his Golinda dearly. He showered her with gold chains and brooches, and

26

caps with ruffles of fine lace . . . things that only money could buy. He added acres to his pastures, and cows to his barn.

"My daughter's married a rich man," Golinda's father boasted, satisfied that she had done well. He never wondered where Gait's sudden wealth came from.

Everyone was glad to see the young couple prosper. Everyone thought them happy. But as the days came and went, Golinda saw that her husband was restless and unhappy.

What could the matter be? she often wondered. How *did* Gait come by so much gold? Golinda watched him with troubled eyes, though she never said a word. She saw Gait change from a carefree boy to a man bowed under a heavy burden.

The song vanished from his lips, the twinkle from his eye. Gait no longer whistled when he dug potatoes, or weeded cabbages and onions. Often, when he thought he was alone, he brushed tears from his eyes.

Soon Golinda noticed that Gait stole away into the night, when the mists swirled through the beech wood and the owls screeched *To-whoo-hoo*. Then she guessed at last what troubled her husband.

"It is the White Witch," she cried in anguish. "It is she who gave my poor Gait his wealth. Now she will hold him in her power forever . . . unless I can break her spell."

Golinda recalled stories she had heard in childhood of the dreadful Witch of Espeloo. Once in her power, she set harder and harder tasks for her beguiled young men until, in utter exhaustion, they died.

"She robs them of their youth in payment for her gold," Golinda sobbed.

But at last the girl wiped her eyes and sat down to think. There was something else she had heard once . . . if only she could remember the exact words. . . .

"If the White Witch ever snares your beloved, *go at once to the Willow Man.* He lives in a tree on the banks of the Yssel. He can help you, my child. He rules the valley where the river flows. His goodness is greater than the evil of the witch."

Some days later, after Gait had gone to market with his vegetables and fruit, Golinda set out in search of the River Yssel and the Willow Man. Once she found the boundary of his kingdom, she walked to the northwest, the direction in which the river lay. The way was long. Golinda was weary. But by afternoon the girl had cov-

27

ered the green valley. Through the willows in the distance, she glimpsed a winding silver thread.

"The river, at last," she cried, speeding her dragging feet. As she drew nearer, Golinda stopped in dismay. "So many willow trees," she exclaimed. "How can I know which is the Master's?"

At that moment Golinda heard a rustling in the great tree over her head. She glanced up quickly, then gasped in amazement. From the fluffy crown of green leaves a man's head appeared. Two bright kind eyes peered into her own. At once she knew that this was the one she sought. Golinda clasped her hands and implored,

> *Willow Man, Willow Man,*
> *Lean down from your tree.*
> *Help me, help me,*
> *Give counsel to me.*

Scarcely had Golinda spoken when the tree began to sway. Almost before she knew what was happening, the trunk was transformed into a man's body, its long branches into arms and legs, its foliage into a long beard. Then she saw a little old man, dressed all in green, from the peaked cap on his head to the pointed toes of his shoes.

He bent toward Golinda, his voice as gentle as the flowing river.

"I am the Willow Man," he said. "You, my daughter, are weary from your journey. Sit down beside the river. Tell me what brings you so far . . . what sorrow prompts you to seek my help."

Golinda poured out her story. She told of her love for Gait, of the danger that threatened him.

"Help me, good Willow Man," she ended. "Tell me how to defeat the White Witch. Gait, already in her power, will be lost to me unless you can tell me what to do. I'd gladly give my own life, if only I could save his."

The Willow Man regarded the girl with his bright friendly eyes. He stroked his long beard thoughtfully. At last he spoke.

"Love such as yours, my daughter, is more potent than magic spells. The White Witch is wicked. She should die. But unless she enters my kingdom, I cannot touch her." The old man paused, pondering his words. "If you are not afraid, Golinda—if you can lure the Evil One across my boundary—I can destroy her. But remember, the witch will kill *you*, should you try and fail."

"I am not afraid," declared the girl. "I'll gladly risk my life for Gait."

"This very night, then," said the Willow Man, "when the wind blows the mist across the valley, disguise yourself as a youth. Slip from the house while Gait sleeps. Go to the boundary line. There await the White Witch. Entice her to cross the border into my land. Only thus will she be in my power. Only thus can the river call her and destroy her in its depths."

Golinda's heart fluttered wildly as she awaited nightfall. When she began to hear the owls *to-whooing* from the beech wood, and saw the fog rolling through the trees, she crept out of bed. While Gait tossed his head in fitful slumber on his pillow, his wife pulled on his breeches and buttoned up his coat. She tucked her shining tresses under his red knitted cap. Golinda stared down at Gait's tortured face. Swiftly she kissed his forehead, then left the house.

"Dear God, give me courage," Golinda gasped as the mist wrapped itself about her like a winding sheet. She missed the path. She stumbled into a tree. The girl felt her way forward, inch by inch. At last she reached the boundary and stood on the Willow Man's land.

To Golinda each passing minute was an eternity. But after a while she heard a soft swish-swishing. She saw a white figure gliding toward her on the mist.

"Come to me, lad—come over here to me," a voice entreated through the haze.

Golinda did not answer. She stood still where she was.

"Follow me, follow me," the voice wheedled.

"I'll not follow you," cried Golinda, making her voice husky and low. "You must follow *me*, White Witch of the mist."

"Tell me who you are, lad," begged the ghostly figure, approaching.

"Come over here. Find out for yourself," Golinda cried.

"But you stand on the Willow Man's land," objected the wraith.

"What of *that*?" retorted Golinda, and took a step backward.

"No, no," pleaded the witch. "Don't leave me. The Willow Man is my foe. If he should see me, he'd have my life."

"Not while *I'm* here to protect you," said Golinda, holding out her hand. "Come . . . it is only one step more."

Unable to resist the charm of the unknown youth, the witch glided over the border on the wind-borne mist. No sooner did she

30

enter the realm of her ancient enemy, than she heard the river calling through the willow trees.

"Come hither . . . come. Rest on my green banks."

She was powerless to withstand the call. The river drew the White Witch forward. Far to the west it drew her, to the place now called Windesheim. There she screamed and fought and fell to the ground in a frenzy.

"Let me go, let me go!" yelled the witch.

She clutched at the branches of the Willow Man's tree on the bank, but he flayed her with his long green arms. He coiled his fingers around her throat. Then the waters of the Yssel welled up. Soon they swirled over the witch's head. They grew foul and black as they sucked her down, down, down.

The wicked witch lies there yet, deep in the bottom of the river bed. And at the place of the terrible struggle, the Yssel is still dark and murky.

When Golinda reached home that fateful night of the White Witch's death, she told Gait all that had taken place. As he listened to her words, she saw the tortured look vanish from her husband's face.

"Your love has conquered the power of the Evil One," he cried, clasping his bride in his arms.

The young couple lived happily forever after, people say. And never again did Gait lust for gold.

MEG O' THE MOORS
(England)

Of England's many witches, old Meg was the worst. She lived in a cave on the Yorkshire moors, near Whitby's holy shrine. Meg bullied the farmers. She blighted their crops. She careened through the sky on a dough pan lid, so many women testified. She howled across the moors at midnight, like a demon in the wind.

When people didn't please Meg o' the Moors—and seldom it was they did—frightening things always happened. There was Farmer Skelton, for one, the night he came home late from the pub. The minute he set foot inside his gate, he sensed something wrong. And when he glanced up at the thatched roof of his barn, the cows were standing there! There was nothing he could do about that in the middle of the night.

"It's all old Meg's doing," he yelled to his wife, as he tumbled into bed. "How shall I ever get our cows down again?"

Farmer Skelton pulled the blankets over his head. He lay shaking with rage until dawn. When he rose, wondering how he would milk the cows, he found them chewing their cuds in their stalls, and his wife tapping her foot at him.

Then there was Ned Grimes, the hired man from Dundry Dip. The very night of Farmer Skelton's mischief, *Ned saw the old witch herself*. She was dancing by moonlight on the moors, dressed in a white shift. Her partner was a fox!

"The selfsame red fox that stole our chickens, and ate the heads off our seven best hens! She'll be the ruin of all of us," blubbered Ned, telling the tale to his friends.

By these things you know that Meg was a plague and a terror to folk on the moor. She did all sorts of horrid things, from riding the mares at midnight and sticking their tails full of burrs to stealing cream from the dairy and turning the bread dough sour.

People were sick and tired of old Meg, yet no one dared do a thing.

"If we ever crossed her, she'd make matters worse," the men agreed, discussing their problem one day at the pub.

"That she would," said Bill Ridden gravely.

He lowered his voice to a whisper, then recounted the dreadful thing that had happened to Mistress Hawes, only a week ago.

32

"This my own wife told me," Bill Ridden began with a sigh. "The Mistress was hanging her Paisley shawl to air, when Meg o' the Moors came by. She'd disguised herself as a gypsy, else Mistress Hawes would be living today.

" 'I've taken a fancy to that fine shawl of yours,' whined the stranger, as bold as could be. 'You'd better hand it over,' she threatened. 'I'd like it for my back.'

" 'Why *should* I give my best shawl to you?' cried Mistress Hawes, clutching the Paisley to her breast.

"The old woman cackled, then shuffled off in a huff.

" 'You'd better watch out,' she muttered. 'You'll find out why, soon enough.'

"It was the next day my wife called to see the Mistress. She was plainly bewitched, said my wife. She wandered about like one lost. When she opened her cupboard and found her shawl gone— though she'd put it there the previous night—Mistress Hawes went white as a winding sheet."

"What happened then?" urged the men, hitching their stools closer.

Bill Ridden sighed. Then he took a sip of ale.

"All at once the poor woman fell down on the floor," he continued, wiping his lips with the back of his hand. "When my wife reached her side, she was mumbling old Meg's name. Barely five minutes later, the poor Mistress was dead."

The men slammed down their mugs and stared in horror at Bill's white face. One man wiped away a tear. The others just sat there, too shaken to speak.

"So now Meg's killing our old folks," Hugh Dansey said at last.

"Next we know, she'll murder our children," cried Pete Jones, father of a newborn baby.

"Yes, and she'll have us *all*, before the twelfth month ends," shrieked Ned Grimes, collapsing on the table.

"You blubbering idiots! You sniveling fools!" boomed young Tom Bowers from the corner, where he sat teetering on the legs of his chair.

Tom scanned the frightened faces, then let out a guffaw.

"So old Meg scares you to death," he mimicked. "Yet not one of you dares stalk her to her lair. You let her rob, terrify, and kill you, yet nobody fights her back. If a stranger should ask me, 'Are

34

they mice or men?' I'd have to confess, 'Sir, they are mice!' And for that, I should hang my head in shame."

The other farmers glared at Tom, a recent arrival to the moors. He was a big burly fellow, with an eye for the girls. Tom's fist packed a wallop. The tongue in his head told tall tales. Yet for all his dash, Tilly, the prettiest girl in the village, had turned him down last night at the dance.

Bill Ridden eyed the young man coldly.

"Since you, my friend, seem to be the only one here not afraid of Meg," he said, "why don't we send *you* out to the moors to get rid of her?"

"Aye, aye," yelled the others, stamping and scraping their feet. "We'll appoint Tom to do the job we 'mice' are afraid to tackle."

"Right-o," Tom cried, banging down the chair legs. "I'll show you it takes more than old Meg to frighten Tom Bowers. *I'll* go after her. I promise I won't be back until I catch the old witch."

In spite of his bold words Tom didn't like the idea of hunting out her den. Yet after his bluster, he had to accept the challenge. He buttoned up his jacket, then stamped to the door.

The men called him back, proposing a toast.

"To our great hero," they jeered, lifting their mugs. "To Tom Bowers, who isn't afraid of old Meg!"

Tom laughed with the others, then mounted his chestnut. He headed straight for Mulgrave Woods, where everyone said the witch had her lair.

"Good luck, lad," shouted the farmers as he clattered off. "All the best to old Meg!"

The horse trotted briskly across the moors, purple with heather, golden with gorse. Tom didn't see the beauty about him, for his thoughts were on the witch and how he would outwit her. He tried to remember all the stories he'd heard about Meg since he had come to the moors. That she was vengeful and wicked, everyone agreed. Some claimed she carried a magic stick, that worked her bewitchments.

"If she touches anyone with it," an old man had said, "it will cut him in two!"

I'll remember that, thought Tom, when I meet the old girl! If I can wrench that stick away, I'll give her a good surprise!

Aware as he was of his danger, Tom couldn't help thinking of Tilly, and the way she had turned him down at the dance. Her eyes were so blue, her hair so pretty as it lay in black ringlets against her white neck. If I can get Meg, maybe I can get Tilly, too, thought Tom. Just then his horse entered Mulgrave Woods.

The leaves rustled under his dancing hoofs. Dry twigs crackled as he flew along the sunlit path. Tom watched sharply from right to left, lest the witch pounce from behind a tree. The young man sat his horse boldly, whip in hand.

"One smack across her ear," he said, "and Meg will drop her stick."

He had scarcely spoken, when a wild screech overhead made the leaves quiver on the trees. The blood drained from Tom's ruddy cheeks. His hair stood on end. Far up in the sky he could see the witch. Seated in the lid of a dough pan, she was bearing down at furious speed. Meg brandished her stick, as if driving a coach-and-four through the air. She was yelling at the top of her lungs.

"So you'll smack my ear, will you? Just wait, my fine fellow. I'll smack *you* and that clumsy horse you're riding. You'll soon find out what it means to tangle with *me!*"

Meg was gaining bit by bit. The horse bolted ahead. He shot through the woods, then bounded into the open moor. Brambles caught at Tom's whip, tearing it from his hand. My only hope of fighting the witch, Tom groaned. He leaned far over his horse. He clutched the animal's mane as he strained ahead. Then Tom yelled, wild with relief, "Water! I see the river over there!"

Tom dug his toes into the horse's flanks. He urged him to greater speed.

"Run, friend, run as never before. The river's our only chance. Witches can never cross water!"

The beast galloped on. He leaped over the moor as with wings on his feet. But Meg was coming closer all the time. She brandished her stick, trying to touch the horse's tail. Tom felt her hot breath scorching his back.

"I'll get you! I'll get you!" gloated the witch.

"But you haven't *got* us yet," Tom yelled over his shoulder as he urged the chestnut ahead.

All the while he was watching Meg from the tail of his eye. When she's close enough, he thought, I'll snatch her stick. She'll have it on our backs in no time if we can't make the river."

"Faster, faster," he whispered in his horse's ear.

The animal bounded ahead. Each second the witch whizzed closer. Her peaked hat sailed away in the wind. Her long gray locks whipped out behind.

"On, on," gasped Tom. "The river is barely seven feet away."

The horse made a tremendous leap. His forefeet landed in the water up to his knees. Tom twisted in the saddle. He tried to grab the witch's flapping stick. Meg screamed in triumph when he missed. Then she brought her stick down on the horse's rump with the blow of a butcher's cleaver. The impact cut the poor beast in two. The hind legs shuddered, then fell into the river. Soon they sank out of sight.

Tom clutched the chestnut around the neck. Again the witch lifted her stick, but before she could strike, Tom tore it from her hand.

"Take this, wretched witch, for attacking my horse," he cried in a rage.

Tom slapped the stick down fiercely on the witch's shoulder, for he could reach no farther. With the sound of a hundred thousand trees splintering apart, old Meg's thin body flew in every direction. She dropped into the river at once. With an angry roar, the waters seized the witch—then dragged her down, down, down.

No sooner had the witch vanished, than the horse's forepart lunged on. Desperately, Tom clung to his neck, and was carried safely to the bank. With a mighty effort, the horse clambered up the steep slope, then died with a sigh. Tom collapsed in the heather, unconscious.

How long he lay there before help came, Tom never knew. When he recovered, he called on Tilly. She didn't turn him down this time when he asked her to dance. Tom was the village hero. With his own cunning—and the aid of his gallant horse—he had slain the witch. She could never terrorize the countryside again.

Soon wedding bells chimed out gaily . . . for Tom and Tilly were wed. They lived happily on the moors forever after. And when Tilly wanted to teach their children how to be brave, she reminded them of their father. He had vanquished Meg o' the Moors, she said. He had shivered her into pieces with her own magic stick.

A WISP OF STRAW

(Netherlands)

This tale is about a wizard who vanished centuries ago from Leeuwarden, the most beautiful town in Friesland. To this day people speak of the wizard, and wonder how he escaped. Some say it happened this way, others say that; but what *really* took place, no one knows.

Once Friesland had as many witches as her cows have black spots. But how to distinguish a witch when you saw one, that was what bothered the men! The girls were all so handsome—just as they are today—that to see them was to love them madly. Yet behind the flowerlike faces and eyes as blue as the sea, many a dazed young lover discovered the soul of a witch.

The men of Leeuwarden were desperate. Night after night at the tavern, they huddled together over mugs of ale and discussed the situation.

"My Betje looks like an angel," Johan told his companions one night, "yet once I saw her on a broomstick, flying through the sky!"

"Well, *I* saw my lovely wife, Cornelia, turn into a hare," confided Wiebe, glancing at the others. "I was going home through the meadow, after a night with my friends. The hare hopped straight toward a cow, and sucked away her milk. I saw this with my own eyes, surely as I'm sitting here. Yet—when I reached home, in a sweat of fear—there lay my beautiful Cornelia, sound asleep in bed!"

"We must do something about it," the men finally agreed. "We must learn how to know a witch, before we wed."

A stranger, sitting in the corner, chuckled.

"How to know a witch—*that*, my friends, is easy if you'll leave it all to me."

The men turned and stared at the stranger who drank alone, his dog at his feet. He was a small bearded man, with spectacles on his nose. He was dressed in black, with a black skullcap on his head. At his side lay a bundle of straw.

"Who are you, stranger?" Johan asked, peering into the corner. "Tell us how you can do this thing."

"Dr. Faustus is my name," the man replied. "I am a wander-

ing magician, well known east of here. I make my livelihood from town to town, by selling my skill to folk like you."

The stranger in black stooped for his straw, then rose and carried it to the table where the others sat.

"I tell you, friends, it will be easy to uncover witches here. I'll do it gladly—if you meet my price."

"Tell us *how*," the men shouted, making room for the magician at the table.

A crafty smile flitted over the lips of the man in black. His small eyes glinted behind the spectacles on his nose.

"See this, worthy citizens," he said, holding up his straw. "*This* is how we shall find out! Tomorrow I'll stand in the market square, the bundle under my arm. All the fair maids and maidens will pass me, as they hurry from stall to stall to purchase their cheeses and bread. Since not a witch in the world can resist straw, those in league with the Devil will step up and draw a wisp from my bundle! All *you* have to do is stand on the corner and watch. You'll soon learn who are your witches!"

The men at the table were silent. Then some cleared their throats. At last they began to argue.

"If my sweetheart takes a straw, it will show me she really *is* a witch," one said.

"Well, at least it will cure this doubt that drives me nearly mad," declared another.

"But what if the wizard is making this up just for gold?" a third ventured.

In the end, Johan spoke for the others, for he sat on the Town Council, next in power to the Burgomaster.

"Dr. Faustus," Johan asked, "what is your price for disclosing our witches?"

"For doing a service like this, five hundred gold florins," said the stranger promptly.

The men regarded each other in dismay.

"Five hundred gold florins is a great sum to take from the city coffers," Johan said at last. "This matter only the Burgomaster can decide."

"Let him decide then."

Nodding curtly, Dr. Faustus left the room with his straw and dog.

Once more the men fell to talking and arguing far into the night. To make known all of Leeuwarden's witches was worth much, they agreed. But to still their gnawing suspicions, to determine which women *were* witches—five hundred gold florins was little enough for that!

In the morning, Johan told the Burgomaster all that had happened the previous night. He told of meeting Dr. Faustus, and of his plan to identify the witches who lurked in their midst.

"What!" roared the Burgomaster, white as chalk. "You'd take gold from our coffers for a wandering wizard! A faker, for all we know, who would trick our wives and sweethearts, and even our young girls into branding themselves as witches! Never! I'd never allow such an insult!"

"But," Johan protested, jerking off a button in his anger, "we thought you'd jump at the chance to—"

"No!" the Burgomaster shouted, banging his fist on the council table. "You and the others are mad. You don't know what you're doing. Catch our women as witches, then drown them in the canal—and all on the flimsy 'proof' of a wizard you know nothing about! *Never,* I tell you, so long as I rule this town."

Sweat stood in beads on the Burgomaster's forehead. His fat white face looked baggy and old.

"Where is this wandering fellow now?" he demanded, rising.

"Why—why, in the market place, I suppose," stammered Johan, afraid of the Burgomaster's wrath. "We were all so sure you would approve, that I told him to go there."

"You did, did you, blundering fool?" the Burgomaster thundered, wiping his face. "Then there's no time to lose. Quick, man! Tell the guards to seize him at once and drive him outside the walls. Post a watch in the tower of the four city gates. Send the man to me the minute Dr. Faustus leaves by his gate."

Johan strode from the room, not daring to disagree. Alone, the Burgomaster sank to his seat and buried his face in his hands.

"My Janke, my beautiful Janke," he groaned. "They would stop at nothing, if they learned *you* are a witch. But I won't let them hurt you, no matter what happens."

Only the Burgomaster knew that Janke was a witch; but others *would* know soon if Dr. Faustus stayed in town. Janke would be the first, surely, to draw a wisp of straw!

When he had married Janke—then a young girl—all he had asked was a smile from those deep blue eyes. He had given her velvets and laces, and trinkets of gold to wear on her breast. Janke looked like a goddess, bright as the sun. By day she stayed at her

41

husband's side. Everyone said she was a perfect wife. But by night she flew away with the Devil. This the Burgomaster knew, but he had kept his bitter secret through the years.

"No wizard shall tarnish the name of my Janke," he vowed fiercely, as he waited alone in the Council Room.

It was not long before a messenger arrived. He saluted the Burgomaster.

"Master," he said, "I come from the North Gate, where I watched all who passed through. Dr. Faustus has just left town. I myself saw him go down the road, with his bundle of straw and his dog."

"Good," cried the Burgomaster, with a sigh of relief. "Take this gold piece for your news."

No sooner had the first watcher gone, than a second appeared.

"Master," he reported, "the magician has just left the South Gate. With my own eyes I saw him leave, his black dog slinking behind."

"What!" exclaimed the Burgomaster sharply. "You, too, swear you've seen him?"

"By the Good Book, I swear it," said the man.

The Burgomaster sat thinking as the messenger turned to go. Just then heavy footsteps echoed in the hall without, and a third watcher burst into the room.

"He's gone, Master, *he's gone,*" panted the man. "From the tower of the East Gate, where I watched like a lynx, I saw the man in black depart with his cur."

The Burgomaster studied his informer, convinced that he spoke the truth. But as he, too, left the room, the West Gate messenger hurried in. The stranger, he said, had just set out from *his* gate. He had hastened down the road, with his bundle and his dog. The man had seen it all, plain as could be.

"It is something I can't understand," said the Burgomaster when the fellow had gone. "*The wizard has departed*—that is all that matters. My Janke is saved from death and disgrace."

How Dr. Faustus could leave the four city gates at precisely the same moment is something Leeuwarden people could never explain. But since the wizard didn't prove that any of their women were witches, the menfolk gradually forgot their fears. Now that centuries have passed, they no longer worry—especially since Dr. Faustus never returned to their town. As for the women, there's not a witch among them today, though their shining beauty still dazzles the men!

GOBLIN BREAD
(Greece)

This is the story of Melena who, though not a witch herself, bewitched her goblin guests with a strange tale.

Melena was a peasant girl who made the best bread in Athens. She worked all night, as bakers do, and while she kneaded dough and patted out loaves, she always sang.

> *Tra la, tra la, tra la, and LA,*
> *Tra la-la-LA, tra la.*

Melena made bread as her mother had taught her, and her fame soon spread far and wide. Her loaves were so tender, so white, so round, that rich man and poor man alike bought her wares.

One Epiphany Eve, the last of the Twelve Nights that follow Christ's birth, Melena had more orders than ever before. Rich Demetrius wanted ninety-nine loaves for his coming feast; Zante needed thirty-and-three; Leira fifteen; and there were the regular customers as well.

Melena's fingers flew as she shaped the loaves and placed them in the oven on a long wooden shovel. The bread soon filled the tiny house with a fragrance and warmth that made the nose tingle. *Tra la,* sang Melena, lifting golden loaves from the oven and putting more in to bake. But she would never have sung if she had remembered the night—and that *she hadn't bolted the door!*

Now except for the Twelve Nights between Christmas and Epiphany—when evil spirits roamed the city at will—no one in Athens ever locked a door. At that one season goblins swarmed through the air and forced their way into the homes of men. The small hairy creatures, who had goat's legs and horns on their heads, lived in caverns inside the earth. Everyone feared them, for once they entered a house, they would drink all the wine and strip the cupboards bare. Even worse, they liked pretty girls, so Melena's mother had said, and tried to drag them back underground with them, to cook and clean and wait on them hand and hoof.

Before this night Melena had always remembered her mother's words. But in her excitement over so many orders, the girl forgot everything but pride in her bread.

"To make such loaves from water, meal, and leaven—that is a miracle!" she cried, standing back to admire her handiwork.

As Melena turned to the oven again the wind whistled outside in the trees. Then the door creaked on the hinges. It opened a crack. Stealthy scufflings followed, then snortings and the scraping of hoofed feet on the floor. Melena didn't hear anything strange, for she was singing *tra la* while she baked.

The door opened wider, one inch, then two. Suddenly wild yells and shrieks filled the small house. Melena spun about quickly and dropped a loaf in terror. Behind her stood a dozen hairy creatures, with horns and hoofs. Their grinning mouths were wide open.

"O—OOO—OH!" cried Melena, shrinking back. "Who are you? What do you want?"

"I am Demos, leader of the goblin band," answered the one whose horns were longest, and he stepped forward with a bow. "Don't be afraid. We won't hurt you."

The door—oh, I forgot to bolt the door, thought Melena in despair. I must try to outwit them, to delay them, somehow, until dawn.

"We have heard of you often, Melena," continued Demos. "Your fame as the best breadmaker in Athens has reached even us, who live inside the earth."

The goblins sniffed hungrily. They lunged toward the stacks of bread.

"Back!" ordered Demos, holding up his hand. Then he turned to Melena and spoke in a wheedling voice.

"We've come tonight, to carry you back to our caverns," he said. "You shall be our Queen forever more, and bake fresh white bread only for us. We'll reward you with gold and silver and gems."

As Demos paused, the goblins drew closer. They joined hands and danced about Melena with stealthy running steps. Then they chanted in high shrill voices:

> *Bread, bread, we shall be fed*
> *Melena's loaves of fine sweet bread.*
>
> *Come, come, come without dread.*
> *We have rare gems for your fair head.*
>
> *Flee, flee, ere the sky's red.*
> *Come back with us,* TO BAKE OUR BREAD.

Although Melena smiled and clapped her hands in rhythm to the chant, she was thinking all the time how to delay her visiters until dawn. Aloud, she exclaimed, "Well done, friends, well done. Your dance and song give me pleasure."

"Ah-a-a-a! She likes our song! She admires our dance!" chorused the goblins. They jostled closer.

Demos picked up the loaf Melena had dropped in her first fright. He felt the bread, sniffed it, then gave it to the goblin at his right. With snorts of pleasure the small creatures passed the loaf from hand to hand, until it returned to Demos. With a low bow he presented it to Melena, then tried to lead her away.

"Wait, wait, Demos!" Melena cried. "Let me finish my baking before I go with you. Dawn is yet distant. You and your goblins have entertained *me* with dance and song. Now be seated while I work. Let me entertain *you* with a story."

"A story! A story!" shrilled Demos, jumping up and down in glee.

"A story! A story!" echoed the goblins.

With grunts and hoof-scratchings they slipped to the floor and gazed up at Melena with round eager eyes.

Melena sat down on a bench near the oven, and began.

"On the night my mother was born, my grandmother handed the baby to me. 'Stop her crying,' she ordered. So I bundled my mother into an old red shawl and took her to the market square. But do you know, the more I tried to calm the child, the harder she screamed? She screamed louder and louder, until—"

"What did you do?" gasped the goblins.

"Well, at last I saw a woman with a basket of eggs," continued Melena. " 'An egg, an egg,' my mother yelled. So I bought an egg to keep her quiet, and put it in her hand. Then for the first time since she was born, my mother laughed. She even sang a silly song!"

"The song!" prompted the goblins, hitching closer in excitement.

Melena rose and peered into the oven, then recited in singsong voice:

> *The proud cock struts,*
> COCK-A-DOODLE DO!
>
> *The speckled hen clucks,*
> LC'LC' KUH-KUH-KU!
>
> *The cock, he stands on one red leg.*
> COCK-A-DOODLE DO!

In the hen's broken nest lies one white egg.
Lc' lc' KUH-KUH-KU!

"Bravo!" shouted the goblins, clapping their hands.

"Just as my mother and I reached home," continued the girl, "my mother dropped the egg, and—"

"What then? *What then?*" demanded Demos impatiently, beating the floor with his hoofs.

"Then," said Melena deliberately, as she placed more loaves in the oven, "the egg rolled and rolled, until it reached the kitchen stove. It broke, and from inside it flew—"

At that moment, from the darkness without, a cock crowed in the distance.

"Cock-a-doodle-do!"

"*Black!*" yelled Demos in anger. "It's still black night! That cock has no business to crow!"

"Be quick, Melena. Go on," he ordered, as the goblins shuffled their hoofs. "Tell us, what was inside the egg?"

"*A hen as big as a camel!*" Melena announced in a solemn voice.

"Oh-oo-ooh!" panted her guests.

"The hen grew, and it grew, *and it grew,*" the girl continued, trying to spin out her story. "It clucked, and it cluck-cl-u-ck-ed, until the roof of the house flew off."

"What then?" cried the goblins. "What happened then?"

"Why, the big hen stuck her neck right out of the top of the house. She goggled this way and that."

Melena craned her neck from right to left, in imitation of the hen's movements. The goblins shrieked with laughter and rocked from side to side. Leaning forward, Melena lowered her voice and continued.

"Do you know, all of us tried to push that stupid hen out of the house, my grandmother, my mother and I? We pushed and pushed, but the creature was too big to budge. Then my mother screamed with rage. The hen couldn't stand *that!* With a flip-flip of her tail and a flap-flap of her wings, she managed at last to—"

Melena hadn't finished her sentence before the cock crowed again, now closer than before.

"*Cock-a-doodle-do!*"

"*Red!*" shouted Demos, shaking his fist in fury, for now pink tinged the sky. "We don't fear *you!* Dawn is coming, but it hasn't come yet! Hurry, Melena, finish your tale."

47

Melena continued her recital with such show of haste that the words tripped over her tongue.

"The hen flew away so suddenly that she carried the sides of the house on her wings. Then my grandmother yelled at my screaming mother, 'Wretched child, see what you've done now!' She beat the baby with a feather the hen had dropped from her tail. But the harder my grandmother beat, the louder my mother screamed. She screamed and *screamed* until the house shook. It was only then that I tossed her a walnut, and—"

"And then, and then—" entreated the goblins.

"And then," said Melena, watching the gray light creep under the door, "my mother grabbed the nut and cracked it in her teeth. Out slithered a green snake, with eyes that glittered like a hundred and three diamonds, and a tail as long as—"

The cock, now in the yard outside, crowed for the third time. *"Cock-a-doodle-do! Cock-a-doodle-doo!"*

"W-h-i-t-e!" Demos shrieked in a hoarse voice.

He bolted for the door, the other goblins stumbling and snorting at his heels.

"The dawn, the dawn," they wailed. "We are undone, undone."

As Melena stood trembling but alone among her piles of bread, she could hear the demons shout against the wind in the distance.

> *Fly, fly,*
> *We must fly*
> *Back to our goblin home.*
>
> *Haste, haste,*
> *We must haste*
> *Back to earth's gloom.*
>
> *In the white light*
> *Of this holy day,*
> *We dare not roam, roam.*

"Tra-la," hummed Melena, lifting her last loaf from the oven. "I almost lost you," she cried, clasping the fragrant bread to her bosom.

"Next Epiphany," she added, as she viewed the golden stacks, "I'll bolt my door against hungry goblins who want to steal my bread —even if they do want me to be their Queen."

48

OLD SAL'S CURSE
(England)

Old Sal's ghost lies in the graveyard, buried in a bottle," Dunstable people tell you, with a nod toward the Priory grounds.

Old Sal had been known as a witch in this ancient English town. She had lived alone in a cottage with her big black cat, a creature "bursting with devils." She had galloped through the sky on a stick for a nag. She had mumbled magic words and cast magic spells. Once Sal had been a harmless fortune teller. But the older she grew, the more often she put the evil eye on those she disliked. Whenever she passed, strange things happened.

"Old Sal's a bad one," her neighbors whispered behind her back. "She has dealings with the Devil—that's perfectly plain."

Gossips wagged malicious tongues. If a horse went lame or a cow stopped her milk, everyone was sure it was Old Sal's doing.

"We should drive her out of town," muttered some.

People gathered at corners to watch the old woman shuffle by. Her jumbled words and furtive glances terrorized them, until they sought out the Prior and asked what to do. The Prior—who was a humbug—didn't like to admit he had no answer.

"I'll say some prayers for you," he told his parishioners. "Only *they* can protect you against Sal's evil eye."

But since dishonest prayers never do any good, the corn still withered in Farmer Piggott's field. Little Barbie Perkins still had warts on her nose. When Mistress Meg fell downstairs and broke her hip, and John Puddlestone's hatchet lopped off his thumb, all Dunstable rose in anger against Sal. This was too much to bear.

"Sal's a witch. She must die," the townsfolk declared.

So they tried her for witchcraft and dragged her to the stake in the market square.

"We'll send you to the place where all witches go," they shouted, heaping the wood high about Sal's feet.

They lighted the pile. They taunted and jeered at the old woman. Then all at once the crowd's yells turned to cries of fear. With a sputter and a sizzle and a wild burst of flame, they watched Old Sal's spirit rise up and up. From the red haze about it, they heard her screech:

Holy water,
Book and bell,
The black powers
Of blackest hell
Shall not destroy me.
I'll come back
To haunt you all
Until you give me
Christian burial.

The townsfolk sank to their knees in terror. The Prior blanched like an almond. He tried to pray, but the words stuck in his throat. His knees quaked when he saw Old Sal's face peering at him from the clouds overhead.

"I'll p-p-pray for your soul," he stammered, though he now was sure that Old Sal was a witch. "Only leave us in p-p-peace. I'll lay your ghost in holy ground."

The Prior said this to get rid of the spirit. He had scarcely finished when it disappeared—with a cackle that sounded like the old woman's laugh.

That very night the Prior stood at the altar and mumbled prayers for the witch's soul. The monks chanted lustily. The candles on the altar burned with clear steady light.

The Prior was frightened, though he tried not to show it. The prayer books trembled in the worshipers' hands.

"Evil spirit, I banish you forever and ever," began the Prior in a loud voice. This was not at all what he had promised poor Sal's departing spirit.

"Forever and ever," quavered his flock, following the Prior's example.

"In the name of—" the Prior continued.

But before he could utter another word, Old Sal's ghost suddenly appeared. It slid through the closed door. It glided up the aisle. Then the apparition stopped near the altar. The red haze that trailed after the spirit swirled through the church. Widow Parsons screamed when her bonnet strings singed on the ends. The sexton winced at the hot breath on his neck.

"You've broken your word," whispered the spirit, so softly only the Prior could hear. "I'll *not* be banished. I am *not* evil. But until you grant the burial you promised, I *shall* be! I'll have revenge on you."

The prior paid no heed to the ghost, now close to his elbow. Instead, he started to chant again:

"In the name of—"

But he got no farther. Before he could finish, the ghost struck his jaw. The Prior reeled, then sprawled in a heap on the stone floor. The monks rushed forward to seize the wraith. It cuffed them until they roared with pain.

"Curses on you, wicked witch," screamed the Prior, forgetting where he was.

He struggled to his feet. He shook his fist in fury. The ghost slid off chuckling, then vanished in smoke.

The return of Sal's spirit set the town in a commotion. Women bolted their doors. They refused to venture out, even to market. Children screamed in terror when mice squeaked in the walls or magpies pecked at the thatch.

"Sal's a worse nuisance dead than alive," complained the men, over their mugs of ale.

In spite of anything people could do, the ghost visited the Priory night after night. The specter terrorized the Prior more than anyone else. It tweaked his cassock. It screeched in his ear. One night the wraith even laid a finger, cold as a tombstone, on his shaven head!

"I'll not leave you in peace," hissed the ghost. "*Never*—until you bury me in holy ground."

"Not in a thousand years," stormed the Prior, too angry now to keep his promise. "I'll *not* have such a wicked creature in Priory earth."

He shot out a hand to clutch the spirit, but it whooshed from his grasp with a scream of scorn. The Prior shivered until he almost dropped the Good Book.

The next night—and the next—and the one after that, Sal's wraith whispered to the Prior.

"When I was alive, I wasn't really a witch. I don't want to be one when dead. Let my soul rest in peace. Then I won't trouble anyone, so long as no one troubles me. But when I'm buried, *I'll haunt any who disturb my grave.*"

A few nights later a palmer—a monk who had been to Jerusalem and brought back his blessed palm—returned to Dunstable.

"*I* know how to lay this troublesome ghost," he told the Prior. "Just leave everything to me."

The next day the palmer entered the Priory all alone. He lighted the candles, one by one. He opened the Book. Then he sat

52

down to wait. Before long, the ghost glided up. It uttered a horrid shriek.

The palmer wasn't frightened. From inside his robe, he drew out a bottle with a long slender neck and a fat round belly. He held the flask up for the ghost to inspect.

"You're a clever ghost," the palmer said. "You bully and badger. You make hideous sounds. You slide through keyholes. You dissolve into smoke. You whiff through bolted doors, as if they weren't there. Yet one thing you *can't* do—of this I am certain. You can't swish into this bottle, turn around three times, and then swish out again. As I'm a palmer, you can't do this!"

"*I* can go anywhere." Old Sal's spirit sniffed in scorn.

"Then prove it—if you dare," cried the palmer, holding out the bottle.

He turned it around slowly until it gleamed like a jewel in the candlelight. With a noisy hiss the ghost stretched out like a string. As though greased, the wraith slithered through the slender neck of the bottle. Once inside, the spirit twisted and squirmed. It turned around once—then twice. But before it could revolve a third time and then slither out, the palmer clapped his hand over the open end. He sealed it tightly with some candle wax, then intoned a few holy words.

With Old Sal's ghost imprisoned, the palmer summoned the Prior, who consented to bury the bottle in Priory earth. He even said prayers for Sal's everlasting peace.

From that day to this, no one has ever dared disturb Old Sal's grave. Indeed, no one now living knows where it is. But just to make sure he won't rouse the sleeping spirit, the sexton never cuts the grass in the Priory grounds.

THE PEEPING SERVANT
(Netherlands)

The Dutch tell of a grievous thing that happened at Utrecht in the olden days. Klaas, a farm servant, told the Bishop that Mistress Geerte was a witch. Thereupon the judges dragged the poor soul to the public square, where they broke her bones and burned her at the stake.

Today Utrecht people still mourn their sin. Now they say that Klaas made up his tale—for he hated his Mistress and wanted her farm.

After hundreds of years it's hard for us to say whether Klaas lied, or whether he didn't. But this is the story he swore was the truth.

Close to Utrecht is Oostbroek Wood, where Mistress Geerte had her farm. Strange things happened there long, long ago. The peasants heard shrieks at nightfall. They saw ghostly lights. Wings swished through the treetops. Tap-tappings came from rocks. The whole place was haunted—every fool knew that.

Today devils, witches and evil spirits no longer haunt the place, but where Klaas planted onions and milked Mistress Geerte's cows, there were weird goings on in Oostbroek Wood.

Mistress Geerte was a widow, with wispy gray hair and two front teeth left in her mouth. People whispered she was a miser, with a sockful of gold. Once Klaas snooped in her cupboard and jabbed her featherbed—but he never found a penny for his pains. He didn't get a chance to hunt again, for the Mistress kept a sharp eye on everything. If he even stole an egg, or slipped away a cheese, the widow always caught him and made him give it up.

Klaas hated Mistress Geerte, though her food was good and he could save some florins from his annual wage.

"Just wait until I pay you back for everything!" the servant muttered at his chores. "*I* do all the work here. This farm should be mine."

Each night after supper the widow sent him to the stable, where he slept in the loft. But before he ever shut his eyes, the youth peeped through a knothole—to see what was going on. He could watch Mistress Geerte through the kitchen window. She would always fetch a candle, then pick up her stick. Next she would climb the

54

stairs to the attic, where she put vegetables to dry. Klaas could see the light bobbing through the tiny dormer window. But that was *all* he ever saw, for soon the candle would go out.

"What *is* the widow up to?" Klaas often wondered. "Maybe she hides her sock in the attic. Perhaps she's counting gold."

Late one night the peeping servant saw something very strange. The Mistress moved toward the window, stick in hand. The moon shone so brightly Klaas could see her well. Through the tiny dormer window, the widow pushed her stick. She held it tightly in both hands. Then *Whoo—whooo—too—whoo—too—oo—* with the shriek of a night owl hooting, Mistress Geerte *flew away through the sky!*

The servant's eyes were popping. His hair stood on end. At first he couldn't say a word, because of the wonder he had seen. Then he shouted, "Mistress Geerte's a witch— a *witch!* Why didn't I know? Now I've seen it with my own two eyes. Now she's away on her stick, *I* can search the attic!"

Hastily, Klaas pulled on his pantaloons and grabbed his jacket. Snatching up an old broom handle, he rushed for the house. I'll have to knock the old hag down, he thought, if she comes back and finds me.

The servant raised the latch and went into the kitchen. In darkness he felt his way up the attic stairs. Moonlight poured through the small window, showing him the peppers and onions drying on the floor. Klaas jabbed his stick among them. He poked in the corners, but couldn't find the widow's store of gold.

"It's plain she doesn't come here to count her wealth," he grumbled.

Then he ran to the window and stared up at the moon.

"If *she* can do it, so can I!" he cried, gripping his stick.

He pushed one end through the narrow window, then held the broom handle more firmly. He shut his eyes and counted.

"One— two—"

Before he got to "three," the boy felt a strong wind tug his body through the window.

What happened next Klaas didn't know, for the breath left his lungs as he whizzed away through the night.

When he came to again, he was lying somewhere—in a heap against a wall. All about Klaas was the sound of strange voices. Although he couldn't open his eyes and couldn't move his limbs, the voices soon took on terrible meaning.

55

"We'll fly there at midnight, a week and a day from tonight," said the first voice.

"Yes, and murder them all, as they sleep in their beds," a second added.

"No, we'd better drag them out by the hair of their heads," a third voice insisted.

"And dump them all under the ice of the Oude Canal!" cackled a fourth, with a shrill laugh.

"Where shall we meet?" inquired another, following an awful pause.

"Right here, of course—at Wijk-bij-Duurstede—where else?" snapped the first voice, in a nasty tone.

Wijk-bij-Duurstede, thought Klaas wildly. So that's where I am! All the farmers turn pale when they speak of this spot. Anyone who gets here hasn't long to live. This is where witches meet to hatch their evil deeds!

With an effort Klaas managed to open his eyes. Then he lay quaking, his heart filled with dread. He was humped in a corner, like a sack of meal. Crowded before him were a dozen witches, with eyes like glowing embers in haggard ugly faces.

Klaas scanned the dreadful scene, than gave a piercing scream. Crouching right there before him was Mistress Geerte!

She turned her head and stared at him, then whistled through her two front teeth.

"So there's my prying spying servant—right behind my back. For this, I'll have his wretched hide!"

The Mistress leaped forward. She would have killed Klaas with her stick, if the witch of the first voice hadn't held her back.

"Sto-o-op!" she ordered. "Let's find out what he wants."

"How did you get here?" demanded a tall thin witch.

"How long have you been here?" a short one inquired, with a threatening scowl.

"What have you heard?" another questioned, raising a wraith-like hand.

At first Klaas was too terrified to speak. Then he stammered and stuttered.

"I—I—ne-nev-er heard a single word," he lied. "The wind blew me through the sky, then d-d-dropped me here!"

"You're a liar!" shrilled Mistress Geerte, and lunged toward him.

But again the witch of the first voice interfered.

"The wretched fool is *here*," she said. "How much he's over-heard we can only guess. Come—back to our business. *Then we'll deal with him.*"

Mistress Geerte muttered and cast black looks at her servant. But in the end, the old crones crouched down again, to plot their crime. Klaas was too frightened to listen. He lay in the corner shivering and wondering—would the witches hang him, or boil him in oil? Or would they hack him to pieces and throw him to the dogs?

After a long argument the witch of the first voice ordered Klaas to stand. In her hand she held a long knife. She means me for the dogs, thought Klaas. But she only said—in a voice like ice:

"You've spied on us, young fellow. You've overheard our plans. Mistress Geerte wants to kill you on the spot. But to spare you—*to always live in terror*—is what we'll do to you."

The youth's knees quaked until he could hardly stand. The witch grabbed him by the arm. She jabbed in her knife until the red blood spurted.

"Swear by the Devil—in your own blood—never to tell what you have heard tonight," she commanded.

"Never—never—*never!*" cried Klaas through chattering teeth, as the other witches crowded round.

"Mind your tongue, young man," they shrilled. "Next time we won't let you off!"

So speaking, they pushed the Mistress forward. She stood there waiting, her back toward Klaas.

"Hop on," ordered the witch of the first voice. "She'll take you to the farm."

Klaas gasped and objected, but it did no good. The witches made him mount Mistress Geerte's back and clasp her scrawny neck. With a horrible yell, the old hag jumped to her stick. Soon they were whistling through the sky at tremendous speed. They went like the wind—straight toward Oostbroek—but before they arrived, Klaas felt a sudden heave.

The Mistress flew up. Then she flew down. She swerved toward the right. She switched toward the left. Klaas felt his grip loosen, though he tried hard to hold on. But before he could clutch the heaving back more firmly, he started to drop—down, down, *down*.

Klaas crashed with a plop into the middle of a bog. Then his body bounced back like a rubber ball. He landed in the tall grass by the roadside. He felt cruel pain in both legs; then he lay in blackness, as if dead.

It must have been hours later—Klaas never knew—that a farmer passed by. He heard moans in the grass. When he found Klaas he carried him home for his wife to nurse.

In the weeks and months that followed, Klaas never told the farmer and his wife that he was Mistress Geerte's hired man.

"One day I'll get even with that old hag," he promised himself.

Time crawled along; but when at last—aided by two sticks—Klaas could walk again, he went to Utrecht. There he asked to see the Bishop.

Now the Bishop was a great man who wore embroidered robes. He had a ring on his finger, a miter on his head. Klaas was a poor farm lad, with straw in his hair. At first the Bishop refused to see him; but when Klaas kept saying he had important things to tell, a brother took him to the holy father.

The Bishop studied the cripple and believed his shameless lies. In the end, they led Mistress Geerte to the stake. Klaas never told the Bishop that he'd been drinking the night he plunged into the bog!

We don't know what happened to the peeping servant, except that he never got the farm. But people whispered—and doubtless they were right—that the witches round Oostbroek never gave him any peace!

THE STONE KING
(England)

In England's Cotswold Hills, a huge upright stone stands alone near the ridge of a green slope. Crimson poppies grow in the grass around this stone, and when cold winds blow over the hillside, their petals fall like drops of blood. Then the elder tree nearby, laden with its black and bitter fruit, seems to mutter. And in the valley below, where lies Long Compton village, the swallows circle the tower of the parish church. They whirl and spin like dancing dervishes, and scream out shrilly the tale of the hill and the stones that lie there.

The village people listen and nod, and gladly repeat the story to curious strangers.

"The stone up there is a king," say the old folk, "and the elder tree is a witch . . . and there . . ." They point across the road to stones in a circle, so many you can hardly count them. "That's the King's army. And over there are the Five Whispering Knights. The Witch of the Hill turned them all to stones."

For hundreds and hundreds of years the stones have lain on the hillside. How they got there no one knows, really. Some say the druids—early Britain's pagan priests—carried them there for a temple. Others claim they were tombs of the shepherds who once lived on the slope.

But most of the folk of Long Compton believe the hill is bewitched! Only when the Witch loses her power will the stones turn back into men. These facts are plain as can be, for strange things still happen on the hill—especially at midnight on New Year's Eve.

When the church bells in the valley chime twelve, the stones hear the sound. They turn and march down the hill in silence. From the spring at the bottom they drink a toast. Then back to their places they march again. This wonder—and others—folk claim to have seen. But the story of how all this came to pass began long, long ago, when a foreign king invaded England.

No one remembers his name, but people say that he sailed from Denmark. He landed on the eastern coast, then marched to the west with his army and his knights. He scattered the Saxon foe before him like chaff, and advanced—a conquering hero—intent upon ruling England as King.

60

"Soon this fair island will be mine, *mine*," he declared to the Five Knights at his side.

White hawthorn circled the pastures like a bride's wreath. The King sniffed the sweet air of spring. He listened to the lark.

"All this shall belong to me," he told his companions. "Seven nights ago, as I slept in my tent, the Wise Woman promised this in a dream, *When Long Compton thou shalt see, England's King thou shalt be.*

"We'll soon reach the spot," the King continued, pointing to a distant hill. "We must cross these downs, then march to the ridge over there. Long Compton lies in the valley below. I'll ride ahead, my friends, while you bring up the army. Meet me at the foot of the slope."

The King spurred his black horse, then galloped away, far ahead of the Knights and his troops. When he came to the knoll he dismounted. He studied the place, then led his horse to a spring.

"We'll rest here, my beauty, and await the army," said the King, patting the animal's shining flanks.

With bright eager eyes he studied the hill.

"When I am King of England," said the Dane, fingering the jeweled hilt of his sword, "I'll build my castle on that summit. Then I can look down on Long Compton each morning when I wake."

The invader laughed softly, recalling the Wise Woman's prediction of glory and power. Dreams of easy victory filled his mind. He paid scant heed to the army as it advanced over the downs. He did not notice that the Five Knights no longer led the troops. Huddled behind the soldiers, the horsemen seemed to argue among themselves.

"Already the King of the Danes imagines himself King of the Saxons," sneered the First Knight.

"Yes, and claims that the Wise Woman foretold his success in a dream," said the Second. "But most likely he's planning how to rid himself of us! Our King will never share victory with his Knights."

"Then we must stop him, before he wins it," shouted the Third Knight fiercely. He waved his mailed fist toward the hilltop.

"Keep your voice down," ordered the Fourth Knight. "Do you want the common soldiers to hear us?" He came closer.

"Tell me, what dark deed ferments in that evil mind of yours?" he rasped in the Third Knight's ear.

"To stab the King from behind," muttered the Third, grasping his dagger.

"No, no!" gasped the Fifth Knight. He drew back in horror. "Of murder I'll have no part."

"That you will, fool," cried the Third Knight scornfully. "Why *not* kill the Dane? Once he has conquered England, he will have no need of *us*. He'll send us home, or exile us to distant castles. He might even slay us to keep power in his own hands."

"But he was ever just," objected the Fifth Knight.

"So far—yes," admitted the Third. "But remember, he has never had such a prize in his grasp. I tell you, friends, *to kill the King* is the only way to be sure *we* share the sweet fruits of conquest!"

"Let him stain his hands with the royal blood," muttered the First Knight in his beard. "Then *I'll* take over the army. I'll proclaim myself King. As for that knave, *I'll hang him for treason.*"

Thus the Five plotted to kill their leader before he could reach the hilltop. But when they joined him at the spring, the Knights smiled at the King. They saluted, then proposed a toast to his victory.

"To England's future King," they shouted.

"I shall lead the advance on foot," said the Dane, impatient to start. "You, trusted friends, will follow me. The army will march in the rear. Keep a sharp watch on every side. The enemy may lurk in ambush. Remember," he concluded, eyes glittering with ambition, "once I gain the summit and see the village in the valley, *I shall rule this land!*"

"And we," whispered the Knights, "be your vassals—unless we prevent it."

Sword in hand, the King strode ahead. He did not glance back. At first the traitors followed closely. But when the King, eager to attain his goal, forgot them, they drew aside.

"When shall we do it?" the First Knight asked.

"Not until he is almost there," hissed the Third. He concealed his dagger in his mailed bosom.

"That's a risk," objected the others.

"No," the Third Knight said with an evil smile. "He would suspect us if we gathered around before then."

As the Knights schemed and plotted against his life, the King leaped forward. It will be easy to gain the top, he thought, growing more confident with every step. There was no sign of the enemy. Ahead, the hill jutted boldly against the azure sky.

"I am almost there!" the King cried. He cast wary glances to right and left. "Seven long strides, and I'll see Long Compton in the valley. Then I shall be the conqueror of England!"

63

He had hardly spoken when the hill began to shake. A black cloud appeared. It wrapped itself about the invader until he could see nothing. Then out of the blackness stepped a horrible witch. Her eyes burned like coals in her ashen face. Her body was twisted and gnarled as an ancient tree. In one hand she clutched an ash stick.

The witch stretched out her arms to block the King's advance. He glared at her with anger and fear.

"*Stop!*" shrieked the witch. "You shall go no farther."

The King lunged at the creature with his sword.

"Stop, foolish King. *This hill belongs to me,*" screamed the witch, who grew taller and blacker before the King's very eyes.

Then in a shrill voice she chanted words that made the Dane tremble.

> *Never shalt thou take*
> *Those seven long strides*
> *To the top.*
> *Never shalt thou Long Compton see,*
> *Never King of England be.*

"Out of my way, Old Hag," shouted the King in a rage. "Stand aside, before I cut you in two. I *shall* be King of England. So the Wise Woman promised me."

He slashed at the witch, but again darkness enfolded him. When it lifted, she still stood there. She waved her stick three times over the hill . . . three times over the head of the King. Then she pronounced her spell.

> *Rise up, earth,*
> *Stand fast, stick.*
> *King of England*
> Thou shalt never be.

> *For threatening death,*
> *For defying me,*
> *Thou and thy men*
> Shall hoar stones be—

> *And I, Witch of the Hill,*
> An eldern tree
> *To stand forever*
> *And keep watch on thee.*

As the witch waved her stick, the King saw the earth heave into a mound on the crest of the hill. He struggled to take the last seven strides, but he could not move his limbs. The blood turned cold in his body. He tried to summon his Knights. He strove to call his troops. The words froze on his lips. He could utter no sound.

The last thing the Danish King heard were the words:

> *Thou and thy men*
> Shall hoar stones be.

The last things he saw were the witch's burning eyes, glaring from her ashen face. The last thing he knew was that he was doomed never to be England's King.

Today all is quiet on the lonely slope where the Stone King stands apart from his men. People say the witch who dwells in the elder tree allows no one to touch the stones without suffering her wrath. In olden times some flouted her power, with dire results.

There was the baker who boasted he could count all the men in the King's army. He made a sackful of small round loaves of bread. The story goes that he carried them up the slope to the stone circle that measures almost a hundred feet across. The baker set one loaf on top of each stone. He counted as he passed from one to the next.

"One—two—three—four—five—six—seven—" until he reached seven times three.

But before the foolish man could draw another loaf from his sack, he fell down dead!

His death should have proved that the cunning of the witch was stronger than the cunning of men. But instead of taking to heart the baker's awful fate, the people of Long Compton decided to move the Stone King. They would take him to the valley, they said.

"We'll set the King up in the market place," the village Fathers agreed, "a warning to all who would invade our land."

It took eight chestnut horses and eighteen strong men to carry the King down the hill. No sooner was he there, than disaster came to Long Compton. People sickened and died. Crops failed. A strange disease afflicted the sheep.

The Stone King was to blame, everyone said. He must be returned to the hill. But this time, the eight chestnut horses and eighteen strong men failed to budge him an inch. The beasts tugged with all their might. They pulled and strained until the ropes broke. One horse fell to the ground and couldn't get up. The only one left that could haul a load was an old gray mare.

"But she's too feeble for such a weight," objected many.

Only their dire need made the villagers consent, in the end, to hitch the gray with the chestnuts. No sooner had they done so, than the horses dragged their burden with the greatest of ease! They took the Stone King back up the slope, where he still stands.

No one now doubts that the witch is in the elder tree—or that she'll remain there. As for the Stone King and his men, they, too, will stay where they are until Judgment Day.

THE DEVIL'S BOWLING BALL

(Netherlands)

A long time ago—when the *Oude Gracht,* or Old Canal, was young —the Devil and his demons haunted the town of Utrecht, one-time fortress of the Faith. To prove this is true, the citizens still point to a boulder, chained to an ancient house. The stone is smooth and grim, the chain about it stout. You can see it at the corner of the street called "Eligensteeg," to the east of the Gracht.

"That's the Devil's bowling ball," townsfolk say. "We've held it captive so many years, he'll never dare come back."

That the great stone is bewitched, everyone is certain. But as always with bewitchments, people disagree.

"Gold lies under it," whisper some, nodding their heads.

But in the entire city, none was ever brave enough to prove it.

"If you can prick it with a needle and draw out one drop of blood," others say, "the witch inside will lose her power."

"That stone was once an altar for human sacrifice," declare the learned Fathers of the Church.

Everyone tells a different story. But the tale most people favor is that the Devil used to hurl the stone across the Gracht. Of course we don't know *all* the facts, but this is how the yarn begins:

The folk who lived beside the Gracht found they couldn't sleep, for there were nightly goings-on that wrecked their peace. They would hear thuds and thumpings, first this side of the canal, then that. Fearful crashings always followed that set the houses shaking and dishes jumping from the racks.

Each night the rich burghers bolted doors and shutters, then lay quaking in their beds. Each night the dreadful ruckus rocked them and drove them nearly mad. Children screamed in terror, until mothers stuffed their ears with wool and pulled the bedclothes round their heads.

One night the Burgomaster, the bravest man in town, vowed he'd learn what was really going on. With nightcap on his head and candle in his hand, he crept to the window and threw the shutter wide. Then he stuck his head out boldly and gazed about.

He saw dark forms flitting through the air. Then—before the Burgomaster could draw a breath—a black ball hurtled across the frozen Gracht and crashed beneath his window like a hundred

67

thousand bricks. Howls of laughter followed. Then everything was still.

The Burgomaster slammed his wooden shutter, his face white as the falling snow. Trembling from the tassel on his nightcap to the slippers on his feet, he sank into his featherbed.

"I saw the Devil and his demons," he gasped to his wife. "They're out there playing bowls! *That's* the crashing thunder we hear every night!"

The Burgomaster couldn't shut his eyes. At dawn he rose and peered into the street. There, on the cobbled pavement, lay a stone that forty men could scarcely budge.

"It's the Devil's bowling ball," he told the City Fathers. "That's what I saw flying through the sky last night."

Day after day the Burgomaster consulted with the Fathers. Night after night they endured the fearful din. In the morning they always found the stone lying in another spot.

"We *must* do something," agreed the Fathers. But *what* to do, no man could say.

At last the Burgomaster told his companions, "This is something only a learned man can decide."

So speaking, he took the City Fathers to call upon the priest.

"You must help us," implored the Burgomaster. "We feel that being a man of God—and of learning—you alone can save us from the Evil One."

Now the priest, who was a scholar, was proud of all he knew. Flattered because the men of Utrecht believed he could outwit the Devil, he promptly said, "Leave everything to me."

But in spite of outward calm, the priest trembled in his heart.

"What if I fail?" he asked himself. "Then I'll be a laughing-stock! But if I don't, then I'll be a bishop surely."

After dark that very night the priest put on his earmuffs and buttoned up his coat. Then out he went into the frosty air and walked along the Gracht. He heard no din and saw no sights. But in time the Devil sauntered up. His bulging eyes glistened like lanterns in the dark.

"Ho, stranger!" he cried out. "Whatever brings *you* here at night?"

"I want to see if you can do three tasks," said the priest boldly, though in his boots he quaked with fear. "I've always considered you clever, but not so clever as I."

"Conceited fool!" roared the Devil. "There is nothing *I* can't do."

His horns shook with rage. Sparks spouted from his nose.

"Not so clever as you," he sneered, switching his forked tail. "Hurry up and state your case. I haven't all night to wait. But first get this inside your empty pate. If I do all you ask, *you'll be mine forever.*"

"Very well," agreed the priest. "But if you can't—"

"That's too ridiculous even to consider," bellowed the Devil. "*I* always win!"

He stamped the ground until the houses shook, and icicles trembled on the trees.

"If I can't do anything *you* think up, my pious, sharp-nosed priest," cried Satan, "I'll leave this town of Utrecht, never to return."

"Agreed," the priest said, keeping his voice steady.

The Devil jeered at him.

"Hurry, priest, tell me what I can't do!"

The priest said, "Count all the icicles that hang in Utrecht tonight."

With a roar of delight, Satan clapped his hands. A host of demons swarmed through the sky.

"Get to work at once," he ordered, hustling them away.

Up and down the Gracht they flew, faster than swarming bees. *Snap! Crack! Bang!* Icicles split and splintered from every tree. *Bang! Crack! Snap!* Icicles crashed to the streets in glistening piles. Then away flew the demons to the house gables, later to the Cathedral tower. They roosted there like bats, and knocked off icicles till the great chimes rang as if it were Judgment Day.

The noise was fearsome, and the priest afraid, for he saw he was losing to Satan. Indeed, the Devil was back, grinning with glee, before the holy man could turn around.

"Utrecht has a hundred billion and thirteen icicles tonight— or *had*, before my minions smashed them," announced the Devil. "So this is the first task I can't do! Hurry, priest, what is the next?"

"Count all the fish that swim in the Zuyder Zee," said the priest. "Perhaps you can do *that!*"

With howls of joy the Devil was off, hordes of demons at his hoofs. But before the priest had said his beads, the fiend was back at his side. He chuckled loudly at the priest's stricken face.

"So *that* was hard, you think?" scoffed Satan. "It was an easier task than the first. In the Zuyder Zee there swim three hundred tril-

70

lion, four hundred thousand and sixteen fish. Quick! Quick, pie-faced priest! Name the third thing you'd have me do. In next to no time now, I'll be carting you away on my back. And then, meddling fool, you'll wish you'd never been born!"

The priest stared into the wicked bulging eyes. He gazed at the leering face, the hoofs, the tail. God is my one hope, he thought. His word can save me yet. Aloud he said, "Show me, Devil, that you can bend your knees. Then recite the Lord's Prayer from start to finish."

At these words, Satan screamed like a wounded dragon. With the roar of a bursting cannon, the Devil zoomed into the air. All the demons swooped after him, and then the priest knew no more.

In the morning the citizens found him, lying in a dead faint, in the snow. Back in his house, when fully revived, the priest related what had happened. All the people declared he was a hero, for he had outwitted the Devil and sent him away.

But the Dutch folk take no chances when it comes to routing evil. The priest talked with smithies and set them to work. Day and night they labored to forge a mighty chain. This they wound about the boulder the Devil had pitched across the Gracht. To the corner of the house they chained the stone, just where the Devil dropped it the night of his last game.

The priest they made a bishop; for surely one who could out-wit the Devil was a very holy man. When he had received his miter, and taken up his staff, the new bishop led his flock to the chained stone. There they lighted candles and burned incense. There they recited the Lord's Prayer. This rite they repeated whenever any thought Satan might be hovering near.

The Devil and his demons never dared return to Utrecht, but you can see his bowling ball—chained to the corner of the house on Eligensteeg, to the east of the Oude Gracht.

THE WITCH IN THE HILL
(England)

In England there's a village that huddles about a strange old hill above the River Flitt. The mound is green all over, from the wide ditch at its base to the broad, flat top, where cows wander to nibble the tall lush grass.

Conger is the name of the hill—some say, because witches from all England once congregated there to plot their evil schemes.

Hetty the witch lives inside the hill, and there she has lived for hundreds of years. When the village was young, long, long ago, Hetty roamed the countryside. Her nasty pranks and thieving ways gave the farmers no peace, for they never knew who would be her next victim.

No one sees Hetty nowadays, for she can't ever leave her hill. But as surely as Shrove Tuesday rolls around once a year, the village children *hear* her, just as their parents and grandparents did.

When the hands of the church clock point to ten minutes of twelve, the sexton pulls the rope of the Pancake Bell. *Tingery, Tingery, ting tang, ting,* it rings. Women hurry to their kitchens to start making pancakes. The schoolmaster dismisses school. With loud whoops the children tumble through the door and sprint for Conger Hill. Up the grassy slope they race. Once on the top, they stoop down and listen, their ears close to the ground.

From inside the mound, as clear as can be, comes the hiss of hot fat—sizzling, sputtering, and splashing from a huge pan.

"It's Hetty frying pancakes," the children shout in excitement. "The Old Woman's making stacks and *stacks* and STACKS for her Shrove Tuesday feast."

"Pancakes for dinner, doughnuts for tea," they sing, satisfied for another twelvemonth, at least, that Hetty is still in the hill.

Then down the green slope they plunge and scramble. They run home as fast as they can, to gobble enough pancakes to last them through Lent.

The practice of listening to Hetty's *sizz-sizzling* while the Pancake Bell *ting tangs* from the church still goes on in the village. No one—not even the very old, who always remember such things—knows how the custom began. Some claim it was this way, others say that, but perhaps it all started with Hetty's horrid tricks.

72

Long ago when the witch roamed at will, she would take whatever she wanted without a by-your-leave. She would snatch pies from the pantry, and tarts from the table—with company coming for tea. She would steal milk from the cows, and eggs from the hens. She'd fly away gloating, with a newborn lamb or a squawking chicken. People had even seen her buzz off with her hat turned peak down and brimming with corn!

Hetty clearly loved to eat. Yet for all her snatching the fattest fish, the richest cream, and the biggest butter pats, she looked like an old bag of bones.

"We'll whip her out of the village if we ever lay hands on that witch," farmers threatened. "We'll throw her over a cliff."

But in spite of bold talk, every man blanched at thought of a skirmish with Hetty.

When youngsters were naughty, all mothers had to say was, "I'll tell Hetty to cart you away on her back." Or, "Hetty will lock you up in her hill, if you don't mind your manners at once."

Just to mention the witch's name so terrified children that they changed into cherubs. To even *look* at the hill scared them half to death. Rather than pass the dreadful place, they all took the long way to school—all except Willie Downes.

Nothing ever scared Willie. He was strong and tall, with a mop of red hair and a freckled nose. He jeered at the younger children's fears. Hetty didn't frighten him. Probably she wasn't even real, he said. Just to show off, Willie crept from his bed one night and walked around Conger Hill three times, all alone in the dark.

"I'm still here," he boasted at school next day. "Until I see Hetty with my own two eyes, I'll never believe she's real."

"*See* her," screamed Evie Gentry, pale to the roots of her yellow curls. "Who needs to *see* her? Hetty's everywhere!"

Then Evie told about her mother's beef-and-kidney pie. She had lifted it from the oven and set the pie to cool in the kitchen. Hearing a hen squawk, she rushed to the barnyard. When she came back, *the pie wasn't there!*

"All we had for supper was cold beans and tea," Evie finished, "while Hetty feasted on our kidney pie."

"What makes you think Hetty took it?" scoffed Willie rudely. " 'Hetty's stolen this,' 'She's snatched that,'—that's all our elders ever say. As for your pie, Evie—how about that tinker who wandered through the village yesterday?"

73

On hearing this, Tommy Browning taunted, "Since you're so sure Hetty isn't real, perhaps you can prove it."

"Yes, yes," shouted the other children, crowding closer. "Proof —that's what we want. Give us proof, or else eat your own words."

"Maybe you'll tell us how that red fox disappeared, after the hounds had closed in for the kill," one boy yelled.

"Or explain the blue lights that flickered over the empty cottage at Prior's End," cried Jack Diston, the weaver's son. "When I saw them I crept to the window and peeked inside. There in the middle of the floor, *I saw Hetty dancing with a broken chair!*"

By now the younger children were shivering with fright, the older ones nervously glancing behind. Willie Downes roared with laughter at their stricken faces, then burst out, "You're a lot of bleating sheep, the way you swallow this twaddle about Hetty's bewitchments!"

"Bleating sheep, are we?" retorted Tommy hotly. "We'll give you until Shrove Tuesday, three weeks from today, to prove *you're* right."

The boys and girls cheered and clapped their hands.

"All right, I will," Willie shouted, although in his heart he wondered *how*.

But when he heard the children's awed "Ohs" and "Ahs" and saw the girls' admiring glances, Willie was pleased with himself.

"I'll think up a good story," he muttered as he raced down the lane. "I can get those sillies to believe anything I tell them."

When he reached home Widow Downes, who sewed for their living, asked Willie to milk the cow. He ran to the pasture whistling. He swung the empty pail over his head, then chased a rabbit to its hole.

As Willie bounded up to Daisy, he stopped short and stared. There on the ground stood a blue jug. It foamed with warm bubbly milk.

"Someone's been milking our cow!" exclaimed Willie.

He peered through the bushes. He searched the pasture. He could find no footprints, no signs of the thief. Daisy stood there chewing, curling her long pink tongue about her cud. Suddenly Willie jumped with fright. His red hair stood on end. Gooseflesh prickled all over his skin. *The jug had vanished.* Where it was standing the second before, a black hare hopped in the grass.

Scarcely knowing what he did, Willie kicked the creature with his boot. A fearful crash followed, like a thousand dishes smashing to

bits. Willie covered his eyes with both hands. When he dared peep through his fingers, he saw pieces of blue crockery all over the meadow. He was standing in a pool of milk.

Willie uttered a yell and fled home. When Widow Downes saw his white face and shaking hands, she thought he had fever. She sent him to bed with a dose of herb tea. She put a hot stone at his feet.

Alone in the dark Willie tossed, turned, and moaned. If he shut his eyes a second, he heard rumblings and mutterings that made him sit up. When he dozed off at last, a voice grated in his ear:

"Willie Downes, you'll *never* prove Hetty isn't real!"

Just then the cock crowed in the garden below. Willie stumbled from bed. He pulled on his trousers, then crept down the stairs, taking care not to rouse his mother.

With fingers that trembled, Willie brewed a pot of black tea. After he had gulped down seven cupfuls, he began to feel better.

"I *did* have fever when I went to bed," he reasoned, "then nightmares the rest of the night."

To convince himself he was right, Willie grabbed his jacket and dashed for the field. Daisy glanced up in surprise when her master didn't greet her. Instead, he dropped to his knees and fingered through the clover. He crawled over the pasture without skipping an inch. Not one fragment of crockery did he find.

With a whoop, Willie rushed to Daisy. He kissed her wet nose. He hugged her sleek neck.

"I *was* feverish last night," he shouted in her ear. "You and I *didn't* see a blue jug, or a hare that broke into bits. There *wasn't* any pool of milk."

For breakfast that morning, Willie ate so much porridge his mother smiled.

"The fever's gone," she said, "thanks to a good night's sleep and my herb tea."

Willie grinned and said nothing. At school, he swaggered as usual before the other children. But all the time he kept thinking what tale he'd invent to show up Hetty for a fraud.

That night in his room Willie heard shrieks and swishings, and this time he knew he had no fever. He stared into the darkness with wide frightened eyes. He thought he saw a form flitting over his bed. He reached out a hand to ward The Thing off, and felt something bony and COLD.

After that dreadful instant, Willie was afraid The Thing would grab *him* if he slept. He didn't close his eyes the rest of the night. At cockcrow he rose, haggard and pale. Even seven cups of strong tea didn't restore his spirits.

"It was Hetty, all right," he admitted to himself, "but I'll never let the other boys and girls know *that*. They'd make me a laughingstock, after all I've said."

When Farmer Todd asked him to help after school, Willie eagerly agreed. What luck, he thought, to get away early and gain time to make up a story!

The first afternoon, Farmer Todd and Willie filled six brown sacks with corn. They stacked them against the barn wall.

"Where I can reach them easily," the farmer said, "when I cart them off to the mill."

That night, and the next, and the one after that, Hetty didn't haunt Willie. He had begun to hope The Thing was a nightmare—*until he saw The Woman in Black!*

She went through the barn door in front of Willie. Then she disappeared. Even though he hallooed and searched the whole place, Willie saw no sign of the stranger. In panic he snatched up a pitchfork. He jabbed it into dark corners. He tossed the hay about. He even lifted the lid of the long tool chest and peered inside.

Satisfied at last that The Woman in Black wasn't hiding, the boy stood still, wondering what to do next. Then he heard a faint rustle. Swinging about, he stared at the row of sacks against the wall.

"One—two—three—four—five—six—SEVEN!" Willie counted.

Seven sacks of corn! Yesterday there were *six!*

Three times over the boy counted *seven*. Then, seizing the pitchfork in both hands, he lunged at the seventh sack. He dug in the prongs with all his might. A terrible shriek suddenly rocked the barn to the rafters.

The Woman in Black burst out of the sack. She darted at Willie with a scream of rage. Later he remembered blood spurting from her leg.

"So you dare say that Hetty isn't real!" cried the witch, waving her broomstick. "Just wait, stupid boy. I'll give you something *real* to remember!"

With that she struck Willie on the head with her broomstick until he fell to the ground, unconscious.

Out in the fields, Farmer Todd heard the commotion. He threw down his scythe. He rushed to the barn—in time, he said later, to see Hetty streaking up into the sky on her broomstick.

"Blood was dripping from her leg," he said. "She was heading straight for Conger Hill. I saw her disappear right into it."

Willie was still in a stupor when the farmer reached him. For days Widow Downes nursed her son. She fed him jellies and soups. But the boy was listless. He refused to get up, even when the doctor pronounced him well.

"Willie Downes is a hero," the farmers all agreed. "He has dared spill the witch's blood."

"And so robbed her of power to return," added the priest, who hurried to Willie's side.

The boy lay in bed, his face next to the wall.

"I'm such a fool," he muttered. "I set out to prove Hetty wasn't real. Now I have proved that she *is*—and tomorrow—tomorrow's Shrove Tuesday."

"So it is, lad," said the priest, striding into the room.

He opened the shutters and let in the sun, then shook the boy's shoulder.

"Get up," the priest ordered. "You still have work to do."

Willie moaned. His head ached. He felt very sick. He burrowed under the sheet. The priest only laughed and dragged Willie from bed.

"It takes a braver man to admit he's wrong, than one who can prove he is right," said the father.

"But I'm such a fool," the boy wailed.

"We're all fools," chuckled the priest, "until we know it ourselves."

Then he drew two straws from his pocket. He placed them in Willie's palm.

"You did a brave thing, lad, in spilling Hetty's blood. People call you a hero. They say you have broken the witch's spell. But *to make sure as sure* she'll never come back, you must cross these two straws on top of her hill."

"Why?" Willie asked, his eyes round with excitement, in spite of himself.

"Because no witch can ever pass the holy sign on her threshold," said the priest.

Without waiting to hear more, Willie rushed from the house. Soon he was climbing the hill. When he reached the top, he parted the long grasses. He groped at their roots until he felt a crack.

"It's Hetty's door," exclaimed Willie in triumph.

He crossed the two straws over it.

"There, Hetty, that will hold *you!*" he cried. "It will teach people never to fear you again."

The next day at school, Willie told his friends, "Hetty's real, all right! I can't prove she isn't, now I have met her myself. But I *can* prove she'll never leave her hill again. Will you follow me up there when the Pancake Bell rings?"

The boys and girls could scarcely wait for the bell to start tanging, so they could dash after Willie. Even the youngest wasn't afraid of the hill with Willie, their hero, to lead them. On top, the children gathered about to stare down at the straws he had laid across Hetty's doorstep.

"She'll never get out now," they shouted.

Then one child cried, *"Listen!"*

They all stooped down, ears cocked for the sound. From deep inside the earth came the persistent *sizz-sizzle* of hot fat flying from a frying pan!

"She's there! She's there!" the youngsters cheered.

Then in high shrill voices they began to chant:

> *Pancake Day, Pancake Day,*
> *Don't let your pancake frizzle away.*
> *Fry it brown,*
> *Toss it in the pan.*
> *There's a real treat*
> *For child, witch, or man!*

Ever since that day long ago, the village children have climbed Conger Hill on Shrove Tuesday to listen to Hetty frying pancakes. No one knows what she does the rest of the year, for she keeps very still. And of course she never comes out. For a witch cannot fly over the sign of the cross, even if it is made of two straws.

THE THREE MISTY WOMEN

(Netherlands)

Long, long ago, three wicked sisters, called the *Witte Wieven,* or White Women, lived in the Netherlands in the woods beyond Lochem. Many thought they were witches, though some claimed they were ghosts. Their home was a *kuil,* or sand hole in the ground. There the sisters quarreled all day. They clawed each other's faces with their long yellow nails. But when the mists blew through the woods at nightfall, they were too busy tormenting others to squabble among themselves. They chased farmers who stumbled home late from the tavern. They shrieked in their ears. They ripped holes in their shirts. Sometimes the witches tripped their victims on rocks— then laughed loudly at their bloody noses and broken ribs. The Witte Wieven never did a good turn in their lives. They made all passersby, except Herbert, quake in their boots.

Herbert was the only man for miles about whom the Misty Women couldn't frighten. He was a poor young farmer, with more courage in his heart than florins in his purse. He always passed the kuil on his way to court Johanna, who lived across the wood. He never hurried, nor heeded the old crones' howls. He only laughed when they rolled stones in his path or clutched at his jacket with their bony hands. Herbert strode along, whistling a merry tune. His love of Johanna left no room for fear.

"Herbert will make a brave husband," Scholte Lodink, the girl's father, often told his wife.

But she only clicked her knitting needles in scorn. She pressed her thin lips together. Johanna's mother was a scheming woman. She wanted her daughter to marry a rich man.

Herbert knew nothing of this until the night Kees stopped at his gate.

"Ho, there," called his friend, "I've news for you." Kees hesitated, gulped, then blurted out, "Across the canal, folk say that old Albrecht is courting *your* girl!"

"Albrecht—that red-faced old fool!" Herbert dropped the roses he was picking for Johanna. He ran to the gate. "Albrecht, with his dangling gold watch chain and embroidered vest! Why, he's old enough to be Johanna's father. She wouldn't look at him twice."

"That's true," Kees agreed. "Her father is against it. *He* wants

Johanna to marry you, because you're a brave lad. But Mother Christine favors Albrecht because he is rich. Yesterday at market, the girl's mother met mine. 'If Johanna marries Herbert,' she said, 'she'll milk cows and weed onions the rest of her life. But with Albrecht she'll be a fine lady, with a maid in the kitchen and gold on her breast.'

"Gossips say Johanna's parents fight night and day, and the girl does nothing but weep."

Herbert was speechless at the news. He swallowed hard, then stared at his snug little house with the steep thatched roof and green wooden shutters. He studied the purple cabbages in long straight rows, the red apples on the trees, the beehives beside the garden path.

Then he thought of Albrecht's grand house, of the curly red tiles on the roof, the tall narrow front, and the gables that climbed up like steps. That house was so fine, thought Herbert in anguish. Why, it even leaned forward to see itself in the canal!

Herbert sighed, then turned from his friend.

When he went through the wood that night, the thought of losing Johanna to a rich old man so plagued Herbert that no whistle came to his lips. His feet seemed to drag. As usual, the Misty Women buzzed past his ears with bloodcurdling howls and horrid shrieks. But instead of laughing them aside, the wretched youth lost his footing. Before he could help himself, he was falling down, down into the sand hole where the three witches lived. Blackness wrapped itself about him like a shroud. Dank air cramped his lungs until he could scarcely breathe.

"Ah-a, we've got you at last!" the youngest sister gloated as she flew into the hole after Herbert.

"You'll never laugh at us again," cried the second, touching his feet with clammy hands.

"Or ever escape us!" the eldest witch jeered, pushing Herbert to the hearth in the center of the hole.

If they guess I'm afraid, everything is lost, thought Herbert as the old hags pressed around with taunts and threats. He really *was* afraid. He remembered his grandfather telling of men who had fallen into the sand hole and never come home again.

Summoning what courage he had left, the young farmer stared at his captors, and said, "Well, now you've got me, what can you do?"

"Do!" shrieked the Misty Women in fury. "Soon you'll see what we can do!"

With that they bound their prisoner with cords of human hair, then pushed him to a stool near the hearth. When the three were weary of twitting and tormenting their victim, they started to quarrel.

"We'll boil him in oil," announced the youngest sister with a leer.

"Indeed, we won't!" the second yelled. "That's too *fast*. We'll drop him into the canal and watch him strangle and drown."

"Stuff and nonsense," shrieked the eldest, pounding the floor with her stick. "Are you blind as bats? Can't you see dawn's almost here?"

For the first time, Herbert noticed the gray light that crept into the hole from the world above. His heart thumped so loudly he feared the old women might hear it. Witches were powerless by day! If he could manage to fool them and break away . . .

The oldest of the three interrupted his thoughts. "Lie down and go to sleep, you two!" she said. "Keep quiet for once."

After more scolding and scrapping, the hags sank to the floor. Soon the cave shook with their snores. Herbert glanced around. Then he tried his cords. The harder he jerked, the deeper they cut into his ankles and wrists. He hitched himself forward, one inch at a time. He held out his hands, hoping to singe the ropes in the fire. Just then an ember clinked to the hearth. The eldest sister opened her eyes.

"Keep still, you fool," she hissed. She rose and hobbled toward the fire. "I admire your courage," she whispered. "You're not afraid of us. I'll help you escape."

With that she cut the cords. Painfully, Herbert rose to his feet. When he tried to thank the old woman, she touched his lips with an icy finger.

"Don't make a noise," she warned, "or the others will hear us. If they do . . . I am lost . . . and so are you!"

So speaking, she gave Herbert such a push that he flew up, up, right through the hole. The next thing he knew, he was lying, breathless and bruised, on a pile of leaves in the wood.

Herbert gulped in the fresh morning air. Then he scrambled to his feet. He stretched his arms. He swung his long legs. Birds chirruped from their nests. Squirrels scampered in the trees. And when the sun rose, the dew on the leaves glittered and sparkled like a hundred thousand diamonds.

Never had the world looked so magnificent—or had it felt so good to be alive. Herbert raced home through the woods, so grateful to the eldest witch that he forgot his worries of the night before. Poor old Misty Women, he thought in compassion, they're not half so wicked as people suppose. And they lead such wretched lives down there in the earth. It's no wonder they have short tempers.

By the time Herbert had bounded through his own gate, and up the path where the bees hummed at their work, a wonderful idea had popped into his mind. *Even witches would like honey cake*, the kind his village had been famed for these hundreds of years. He would get Klees' mother to bake one, such as she alone could make. He would leave it for the witches, beside their sand hole.

News travels fast in country places. By nightfall everyone in the village knew about Herbert's escape from the Misty Women. Kees rushed over to see his friend after work.

"Everyone, including Johanna's father, is boasting of your courage," cried Kees, slapping Herbert on the back. "Johanna would fly into your arms this minute. But her mother, who forbids her to even mention your name, praises Albrecht with every breath."

"It wasn't my courage, but the old hag's help, that got me out of the hole alive," said Herbert truthfully.

After telling his friend everything that had happened, Herbert spoke of the honey cake.

"Do you think your mother will make it?" he asked.

A few days later Herbert saw his friend coming across the fields. He was carrying something covered by a large white napkin. My cake, thought Herbert. He dropped his hoe and rushed to the gate.

"Just look at this, lad," cried Kees. He lifted a corner of the napkin.

There on a large plate was a wonderful brown loaf. It bulged with raisins. It smelled of honey and spice. On top were flowers, fashioned from almonds and sugared fruits.

Herbert shouted with excitement. He sniffed the cake's fragrance. He stuffed a crumb in his mouth.

"Mmm-mm-m-m!" he exclaimed, smacking his lips. "It's the finest cake ever made! If the Misty Ones don't gobble it, call me a fool."

Herbert could hardly wait to finish his chores and deliver his gift. The cake was so handsome, the young man so gay, that he whistled and laughed all the way to the woods.

When Herbert arrived at the kuil, everything was quiet . . . no shrieks in the air . . . no lights in the trees . . . no cold fingers clutching from behind! The sisters won't trip me up tonight, thought

83

Herbert, not while I'm holding this cake. He set down his offering beside the hole, then hurried on to Johanna.

Outside the farmhouse Herbert saw a black horse tethered to a tree.

"Well, you're a fine creature," he said, rubbing the animal's nose and slapping the shining flanks. "You look like a racer to me."

Just as the youth was wondering who the horse's master might be, Johanna threw open the door and rushed into his arms.

"Herbert, Herbert," she sobbed. "Save me from that dreadful old man."

She means Albrecht, thought Herbert with a pang. But before he could answer, Johanna's father was beside him, grasping his hand.

"You're a brave fellow," said he. "One day I hope you will be my son."

"And I hope so too," Herbert said, gazing into Johanna's cornflower-blue eyes.

"Well, *I* have something to say about that," cut in a sharp voice from the doorway.

There stood Mother Christine in her best white fluted cap and black silk apron.

"Johanna is a foolish girl," she said. "She doesn't know what's good for her, any more than her father. My husband and I can't agree on the man she will marry. But we *have* agreed on a test to find out."

The woman's thin lips curled in malice as she explained the nature of the test. In four weeks and a day, Herbert and Albrecht were to appear on horseback. They were to race to the Misty Women's hole.

"Each of you will carry an iron spit," she concluded. "You must thrust it into the kuil. The man who does so, and returns first, shall win our daughter's hand."

Herbert was too dejected to whistle when he went home through the woods. I have lost Johanna, he thought. That tricky Mother Christine knows *my* horse is an ambling old nag, while Albrecht's is a racer!

The weeks dragged by—one, two, three, then four.

"Just one day more before the race," Herbert told Kees. "I have tried and *tried* to make the old mare run. But her running days are over now. Her knees are stiff, her feet like clods of earth."

"Never mind," said Kees with a confidence he didn't feel.

84

"*Anything* can happen tomorrow. You haven't lost the race yet. Albrecht's horse is swifter than yours, but his master is a coward. He might die of fright before he ever reaches the witches' hole. Why, Albrecht has never even dared go inside the wood!"

The following day the whole village turned out to watch the race. Albrecht pranced up on his spanking black steed. The creature stepped proudly. He tossed his shining mane. But his master's face was ashen. His body slumped in the saddle like a sack of meal. The iron spit trembled in his fat jeweled fingers.

No one, except Mother Christine, had a kind word for Albrecht. But when Herbert plodded up on his gray nag, the villagers cheered and clapped. They threw their caps into the air.

"Good for you, lad," they shouted. "We are counting on you to win this race."

That's a joke, thought Herbert. He waved to the crowd, though his heart was like lead. He threw a kiss to Johanna. The mare wheezed and lurched into place beside the pawing black.

The burgomaster gave the signal and the race began. Albrecht's horse bounded ahead. He was in the wood before the feeble nag had gone ten paces. Then everyone beheld a strange thing. Albrecht's swift mount began to slow down. He seemed scarcely to move, in spite of his master's lashings and yells. The mare leaped forward like a frisky colt. She dashed past her rival with a neigh of triumph. She flipped her sparse tail. Then she tore through the wood. She didn't stop until she had reached the White Women's hole.

"Well done, faithful friend," cried Herbert, patting the nag's bony neck. He bent down and slipped his spit into the opening in the sand. "Now take me back to Johanna," he whispered in his horse's ear. "Help me to win my bride."

They had scarcely started back through the wood when something, hurtling through the air, crashed at the horse's feet. Herbert leaned from the saddle to peer at the ground.

"Why, there's my cake plate," he exclaimed. He reached down and picked it up. "It's still sticky with honey." The moment Herbert's fingers closed on the rim, the crude earthen plate turned to pure gold!

"Oh, thank you, dear Misty Women. Thank you for your wedding gift," shouted Herbert over his shoulder, for already his mare was bolting through the wood.

They passed Albrecht as they dashed along. He was thumping his black horse, shouting abuse. The handsome creature was hanging his head. Plodding along like a tired farm horse, the animal was barely halfway to the hole.

When the villagers saw Herbert galloping back, they shouted and jumped in a frenzy of joy. And when the young rider waved his gold plate, Johanna's mother never opened her mouth.

When Herbert had sold the witches' present for a fine sum, he told his Johanna, "This is our golden nest egg."

After the wedding Scholte Lodink reminded Mother Christine, "Now we have a son who is *both* rich and brave!"

Herbert and Johanna lived happily ever after in the snug little house with the steep thatched roof and shutters of green. Nobody remembers *what* happened to Albrecht. The Three Misty Women vanished, people say, shortly after they had eaten the honey cake. At least they never tormented passersby again, in the woods beyond Lochem, where you can still see their hole.

THE BEWITCHED COURT

(Wales)

In East Wales there's a mysterious pool that everyone knows is bewitched. *Llyncleys*—which means, in Welsh, "the swallowed court"—is the name of this pool. Long ago its dark waters swallowed a palace, a king, and a court. Today all lie buried in the mud of the mere, where the yellow flag weeds and green rushes grow.

"The curse of a witch betrayed brought this grievous thing to pass," people say.

Then they tell the story of Evan the King, who once lived in the palace on the site of the pool. The palace, they say, was of dazzling beauty. It had steps of white marble and gold weathercocks. The windows gleamed and sparkled like a hundred thousand gems. Nightingales sang in the pear trees at dusk. All day blue peacocks strutted in the garden, where jasmine scented the air.

In this palace King Evan held his court, and his reign was just and good. At his side sat Queen Mari, whose face was the fairest in Wales. Her long hair shimmered like threads of spun gold. Her lips were like a red cherry, her eyes like violets in May. The King loved Mari madly. He showered her with rubies and diamonds and pearls. Yet all the jewels in the world could add nothing to the beauty of the Queen's shining face.

One might suppose the King the happiest of men. But he was not, for secretly he was sorely troubled by a mystery that surrounded his beloved wife. One night out of every seven, she vanished from the palace. Where did she go? What did she do? Why did she never tell her husband, the King? Such were the questions that weighed upon Evan's heart.

Nine years came and went. With each passing year Mari grew more lovely, but the King watched his wife with fear clutching at his heart. At night he tossed and turned in his golden bed. He brooded alone when the Queen left his side. Yet she only smiled when she went away. Evan dared not ask whither she went.

The day came at last when the King could no longer endure his fears alone. In secret he sent for Wylan the Wizard, his chief adviser at court. Wylan was a man of learning and cunning. He could read the signs in the stars. He could recite magic spells. Surely the wizard would have power to help him, thought the King.

"Wylan," he said, as the wizard bowed before him, "after nine years of silence I must reveal a secret . . . else I shall die of the pain that gives me no peace. But should you violate my confidence, *I shall slay you with my own hand.*"

The old man bowed until his white beard swept the floor.

"Have no fear, Sire," he said. "Long before you were born I served your father. With him I shared dark secrets of state. I never failed him. I shall not fail his son. Let me help you, at least advise, on the matter that breaks your heart."

"It is the Queen," said the monarch. He dropped his voice to a whisper. *"Mari is a fairy!* She belongs not to this world, but to the kingdom of spirits who live inside the earth. This I knew when I wooed her. But I loved her so, nothing mattered but to make her my wife."

The King sighed deeply, then fell silent.

"And now, Sire, are you sorry?" Wylan prompted.

"No," cried the King fiercely. "I love Mari as never before. I would wed her a thousand times over, even on her own terrible terms."

Again Wylan waited for the King to continue. But the monarch sat on his throne, his face buried in his hands.

" 'Her own terrible terms,' " the wizard repeated softly. "Tell me, what do you mean? Where did you meet Mari? How do you know she's a fairy? It may be, Sire, you are wrong."

"No, not wrong." The King spoke as if to himself. "It was when I was hunting . . . nine years ago . . . out on the heath. I galloped past her. She was dabbling her toes in the stream that flowed close to a cave in the rocks. Her hair was a golden mist in the sun. She smiled into my eyes as I dashed after the fox. It took refuge in the cave. I didn't pursue him. Instead, I wheeled my horse around. I returned to the girl."

The King wiped his brow. Then he continued.

"We sat beside the stream until sundown. I told Mari I loved her. I held her tiny hands in mine. I begged her to be my Queen. I could see that the girl loved me, but for some reason she hesitated. After a long time I learned why.

" 'If I marry you,' she said, 'it must be on one condition—that I leave you one night in seven. You must promise *never to ask where I go.* If you do, if you follow me, or reveal my secret to anyone, ruin will come to us both.'

" 'But why, tell me *why*,' I pleaded.

" *'Because I'm a fairy!'* Mari said softly, searching my face with those deep violet eyes.

"In the end, I wed her without further question. And now, nine years later, I have betrayed her, because I have no peace," cried the King in anguish. "You, Wylan, are the only one who can help me. You must devise a charm to break the spell that takes Mari from me."

An expression of cunning flitted across the wizard's sharp features as he studied the King's bowed head.

"Come, come," coaxed the old man soothingly. "You must not despair. Set your heart at ease, my King. I, Wylan, am here to serve you, though it cost my own life. Tell me what to do."

"Follow the Queen tonight," commanded the King, too desperate to note the greed in the wizard's face. "Follow her when she leaves the palace gates at midnight. Take heed she doesn't suspect you, or all will be lost. See where Mari goes. Observe what she does. Then work some magic to keep my fairy wife from leaving me again."

"What you ask is dangerous," declared Wylan after a pause. "If I should fail—but I won't even consider *that*. My life is at stake, Sire, but I shall find a way. Worry no more about your Queen. Leave everything to me."

"Please start at once," cried the King impatiently when the wizard made no move to leave the chamber.

"A man of learning must live," Wylan said, clearing his throat. "The risk, as I have said, is great."

"Name your price, then, and get on with your work," shouted the King. "You have much to do before midnight."

"Should not the price equal the risk of the mission?" asked the old man, eyes glittering with avarice. "To accomplish this perilous task, I shall require one thousand, one hundred and seven pieces of gold, and one out of every ten cows born with black spots."

"So be it," cried the King in disgust. "Do not haggle with me when the matter at hand is so important."

He waved his hand in dismissal, then fell back, brooding, on his throne.

That night Wylan hid behind a tree until Mari left the palace and slipped through the great golden gates. He followed quickly as she sped across the heath. Heading toward the hills, she glided faster and faster. The wizard knotted his long robe about his waist, then followed the Queen at a distance. He sprang over rocks. He leaped across gullies. The slim figure in white moved swiftly until it came to a stream.

Mari skirted the water. When she reached a cave in the rocks nearby, she hesitated. Then she disappeared.

"Aha," panted Wylan, not far behind. "*That's* where she goes! She enters the cave to the underworld, where the evil fairies live."

The wizard sat down on a rock near the cave. To entice Mari out with a spell will be easy, he thought. Then I must bewitch her, so she can never return to the spirit world. That takes more skill, *but I can do it!* After tonight I shall be a rich man . . . *rich.* And now, with the King in my power, he'll not dare order me about.

So the wizard gloated over his good fortune, too sure of his own cunning to dream he could fail in his task. He stretched his tired limbs. He rested his old bones. Then he turned toward the cave and started to chant:

> *Come forth, lovely Queen,*
> *Come out of your cavern.*
> *Let me gaze on the face*
> *That enchants all men*
> *And enslaves them forever*
> *To the fairest on earth.*

Wylan had barely finished the magic words when a horrible witch whistled out from the mouth of the cavern. With a hiss she snatched the sorcerer from the rock. She wound her long fingers about his throat.

"So it's Wylan the Wizard," she shrilled, squeezing his neck until his tongue lolled out and his eyes popped from his head. "*You* followed me here tonight. *Look* at me," she continued, flinging the wizard from her so violently he fell to his knees. "Look at me. I am Mari . . . 'the fairest on earth.' The King has betrayed me. And you, old man, you have discovered my secret."

"*You* . . . Mari!" Wylan gasped, recoiling in horror. Gazing at the hideous toothless hag, the wizard could feel his magic powers ebb away.

"Yes, Mari," mocked the witch with a dreadful laugh. "For six days out of seven, the loveliest woman in Wales. But on the seventh night I must return to the underworld, where I am transformed into the revolting creature you see before you. Now that my own husband has betrayed me, I can never again assume human form. In punishment for his crime, I shall drown him, together with all his court.

"As for you, skulking creature of the night," cried the witch, turning on Wylan with fury, "death is too good for you! Your punishment is to be chained to my side forever."

Speaking thus, the witch seized the wizard's long beard. She dragged him, screaming and struggling, into the cave. She pulled him behind her down, *down,* DOWN to the underworld, where only the wickedest fairies dwell.

Of the King's fate you already know. He and his court and his beautiful palace—with the white marble steps and the gold weathercocks—all sank to the bottom of Llyncleys Pool. Today dark waters flow over Evan's proud head. Such is the curse of the fairy wife his uneasy love betrayed.

THE AUTHOR

DOROTHY GLADYS SPICER has gathered these strange tales of enchantment and spells from many lands. This is her second book for Coward-McCann. Her first, *46 Days of Christmas,* is the story of how Christmas is celebrated in many countries.

The author lives in White Plains, New York.

THE ARTIST

SOFIA has captured the enchantment of *13 Witches* in her outstanding illustrations. The artist lives in Pittsfield, Mass.